Scariest
Stories

Scariest Stories

Ever Told

Roberta Simpson Brown
"Queen of the Cold-Blooded Tales"

Published 2016
by August House, Inc.

Atlanta, Georgia
augusthouse.com

ISBN 978-1-939160-99-7

Cover design: Chris Thompson Design
Book design: H. K. Stewart

Manufactured in the United States
10 9 8 7 6 5 4 3 2 1

Library of Congress Cataloging-in-Publication Data

Names: Brown, Roberta Simpson, 1939- author.
Title: Scariest stories ever told / by Roberta Simpson Brown.
Description: Atlanta, Georgia : August House, Inc., 2016. | Summary: An
  anthology of spooky stories, divided into such categories as "Something's
  Not Safe at School," "Shadows in the Woods and by the Water,"
  "Welcome to Your New Home," "Don't Stray Too Far from Home," and
  "Better Not Mess with What's Best Left Alone."
Identifiers: LCCN 2016021751 | ISBN 9781939160997 (pbk. : alk. paper)
Subjects: LCSH: Horror tales, American. | Children's stories, American. |
  CYAC: Horror stories. | Short stories.
Classification: LCC PZ7.B816923 Sc 2016 | DDC [Fic]--dc23
LC record available at https://lccn.loc.gov/2016021751

This book is printed on archival-quality paper that meets re-
quirements of the American National Standard for
Information Sciences, Permanence of Paper, Printed Library
Materials, ANSI Z39.48-1984.

To my husband,
Lonnie E. Brown (an excellent writer himself),
who gives me love and support

and

To my first cousin,
Arnold Eugene Simpson (always like a brother),
who is truly the greatest storyteller of us all!

I love you guys!

Contents

Welcome to Your New Home

Things Aren't Always What They Seem

Better Not Mess with What's Best Left Alone

Acknowledgments

Thanks to Steve Floyd and all the staff at August House who made this book possible.

Thanks to my husband, Lonnie, who proofed my work and made excellent suggestions.

Thanks to family, friends, and Salvador Doggie who inspired me to write spooky things.

Introduction

We all fear something. It is a universal feeling we share. We like to be scared because it is exciting and fun. The great thing about reading or telling scary stories is that we can control the fear if it gets too intense. We can close the book or cover our ears until our courage builds up again.

I grew up in a time when reading books and telling stories provided excitement and entertainment. To my family, friends, and me, scary stories provided food for our imagination. Sharing scary stories helped us identify our own fears and deal with them. Storytelling was an important part of our lives and is still an important part of our culture.

I wrote these stories for fun. I hope you will enjoy them and pass them along to your friends. Just to be on the safe side, maybe look over your shoulder from time to time to verify that these really are *only stories!*

— Roberta Simpson Brown
Queen of the Cold-Blooded Tales

Something's Not Safe at School

Scales

Jamie Miller had such a strong feeling that he should skip school that day that he tried to fake a bellyache. After a quick check for a fever and soreness, his father put him on the school bus and sent him on his way. The bus unloaded the kids at the front door, and Jamie was swept down the hall by the flow of students.

If only I didn't have old Miss Wilson first period! Jamie thought. *That old woman should have retired years ago. She is going to bore somebody to death before she leaves here.*

Jamie had liked science classes before he came to middle school. He had only become bored with them now because Miss Wilson thought science should only be taught from textbooks and never with hands-on experiments. To liven things up, Jamie had devised ways to entertain the class for the three weeks since school started.

Miss Wilson had received frogs, snakes, insects, lizards, and fish from the board of education, and they were in various containers and aquariums at the back of the classroom. She never incorporated them into her lesson plans. She had arranged for the custodian to feed them because she wanted nothing to do with the scaly, slimy creatures. She was glad she had only this year left before retirement because teaching methods were changing so quickly that she couldn't keep up. She knew her nerves would never stand another year with a student like Jamie Miller. Their mutual dislike of each other had been growing since day one.

The first week had passed without incident, but she had taught long enough to know when a student wasn't on task with her program. Jamie Miller was up to something as sure as she was at her desk teaching. It was just a matter of time, and the time came sooner than she expected. She walked into her classroom one morning after performing her hall duty and found her class in chaos! Frogs were hopping everywhere, and students were making wild leaps, trying to catch them. She called security, and most of the period was taken up by returning the frogs to their containers.

"Who let the frogs out?" she demanded to know.

The class remained silent.

"I am going to punish all of you if the guilty party doesn't confess!" she threatened.

Of all the unfair things Miss Wilson did to her students, this practice of punishing everybody irked Jamie the most.

She is too lazy to figure out who the guilty person is, he thought. *She takes the easy way out and makes everybody pay. She's just mean enough to punish my friends for something I did!*

He couldn't let that happen. The whole class knew he had done it. Even though they would never tell Miss Wilson that he was the guilty one, they would not appreciate it if he let them all be punished in order to save himself. He raised his hand and spoke up without waiting for Miss Wilson to call on him.

"Miss Wilson, I did it," Jamie said. "It was an accident, though. I tripped and fell and knocked the top off the aquarium. They all started hopping out. I'm sorry."

"Report to the principal right now, young man," she ordered. "I do not believe for a minute that this was an accident."

Miss Wilson thought she might be rid of this disruptive little boy for the day, but in a very short time, Jamie returned to class with a pass from the principal.

"She believed me," said Jamie. "She told me to be more careful."

Miss Wilson was furious, but she only told Jamie to go to his seat and to catch up with the class by answering the questions at the end of chapter three in the text.

Jamie sat down and began his work, but he vowed he would take the principal's advice and be more careful.

In the following days, several unpleasant incidents took place that could not be traced to Jamie. There was not a doubt in Miss Wilson's mind, though, that Jamie was the culprit. A fish ended up in Miss Wilson's cup of coffee, a lizard jumped out of her desk drawer when she opened it, a spider crawled across her desk when she returned to her chair after passing out some papers, and one day a bug somehow got tangled up in her hair. Jamie looked innocent, but he savored every moment of Miss Wilson's distress. He saved his best prank for Thursday.

Jamie had noticed that of all the animals and insects, Miss Wilson feared the snakes most of all. She shuddered when she saw them, and she always said she wished she could get those

scaly things out of her room. Jamie would much rather have
her out of the room, and he snuck back into the room after
school Wednesday to put his plan into action. He carried three
rubber, life-like snakes in his pocket.

Jamie had watched Miss Wilson's daily routine. It never
varied. She would close the door after hall duty, walk to her
desk and open the top drawer to take out her roll book to
check attendance, and then sit in her chair while she gave instructions for class work. Jamie knew exactly where to place
the fake snakes.

Jamie hurried home, thinking he would be happy to go
to science class on Thursday. His mother noticed him smiling
several times at breakfast and asked his dad later if he knew
why. Neither had an explanation, but they were both pleased
that he seemed eager to go to school for a change.

Jamie sat in class hoping his plan would pay off. He had
placed one snake on a hook on the coat rack behind Miss
Wilson's chair. He had laid one on the bottom of her chair and
put the third in her desk drawer. The hall cleared and Miss
Wilson closed the door and crossed to her desk. Time stopped.
Jamie held his breath, hoping things would work out.

Then everything happened in quick succession. Miss
Wilson opened her desk drawer for her roll book and saw the
coiled rubber snake. Her face turned white, and she sank down
onto her chair, only to shoot back up when she realized she had
sat on a snake.

She shoved the chair backward with her legs as she tried
to move away and knocked the third snake down on her head.
The class sat stunned as their teacher, who was never at a loss
for words, fainted and crumpled silently to the floor.

The class did not remain silent, though. The boys and girls screamed and shouted for help. Security, teachers, the principal, and the school nurse came running into the room. By this time, Miss Wilson had opened her eyes. The nurse and the principal managed to get her to her feet and support her as she walked toward the office.

Miss Wilson looked at Jamie Miller and spoke for the first time.

"One day, young man, the Scales of Justice will tip, and you will get what you deserve!" she told him.

All eyes looked at Jamie. He shrugged as if he had no idea what she meant.

"Maybe she's in shock," Jamie commented as they led her away.

Maybe she was, because she didn't come to school on Friday.

"Miss Wilson is resting and will be back soon," the principal said in the morning announcements. "The fright gave her a mild heart attack. We should all pray for her recovery."

The students sat waiting to see who their sub would be. Even Jamie was curious.

The door opened and in walked a strange-looking woman who appeared to be a few years younger than Miss Wilson.

"I am Miss Hesston, your sub for the day," she announced.

It's creepy how she hissed when she said her name, thought Jamie. *And her eyes are slanted funny.*

His attention was drawn away from her eyes by what she was saying.

"We will have hands-on activities today," she informed the class. "You will all get a chance to handle the snakes, frogs, and lizards."

The class was the best science class he had ever had! When the period ended, all the kids, including Jamie, were wishing the sub could be their permanent teacher.

As they were filing out, Miss Hesston called out to Jamie.

"Could you report back to me after school? You were so good with the animals that I thought you might help me clean their containers."

"Sure," said Jamie, surprised but flattered by the sub's unusual request.

After the last class, Jamie rushed to the science room. Miss Hesston was sitting at the desk.

"Please close the door, Jamie," she said, smiling at him. "If an animal should get loose, we wouldn't want it to get out of the room, would we?"

"Oh, no!" said Jamie, pulling the door closed behind him. But as soon as he closed it, he knew he had made a big mistake!

Suddenly the room turned cold, and uneasiness crept over Jamie.

"Maybe the custodian turned the temperature down," he said silently to himself.

He knew that was not true, though. This was not a natural cold. This cold was like nothing he had ever felt before. He felt frozen, like he couldn't move, and he could only stand there to see what was going to happen.

"We'll start with the snakes, Jamie," Miss Hesston said. "Let's go over by their tanks."

She is hissing again, thought Jamie. *And she is looking at me with those weird eyes.*

He suddenly realized he had to get out of there. He used the first excuse that came to mind.

"Miss Hesston," he said, "I just remembered I was supposed to go straight home today to help my dad. I've got to go. I don't have time to help you today."

Jamie turned toward the door, but Miss Hesston moved like a flash and headed him off.

"You had time to play cruel tricks on poor old Miss Wilson, though, didn't you?" she asked him.

Jamie's mind had a hard time taking in what was happening. He was alone with some strange creature. This wasn't a teacher. It couldn't be. Whatever this thing was, it definitely meant him harm. He looked around the room for a way out, but this inhuman thing was blocking the only exit.

Why didn't I tell someone where I was going? Why didn't I bring somebody with me? How will anybody be able to help me? he thought frantically. *This is not right! Why is this happening to me?*

"There is justice in the world, Jamie. This is the time for tricks on you," laughed Miss Hesston. The laugh held evil, not joy.

Then he realized that tops were sliding off containers, and snakes were slithering across the floor.

"No!" screamed Jamie. "They were only tricks for fun! Let me out!"

He tried to dash around Miss Hesston, but she grabbed him by the shoulders and flung him to the floor. As he landed, he saw Miss Hesston's sleeve slide up and expose the thin scales that covered her arm.

Jamie tried to get up, but he was too dizzy to stand. The snakes were crawling over him now.

Outside the room, silence settled over the school. The last person left for the weekend. In her hospital room, Miss Wilson unexpectedly started to feel much better.

Don't Open That Locker

As soon as Nora walked through the front door, she knew there was something terribly wrong with her new school. It wasn't just the fact that a girl had disappeared here last year and never been found; it was the uneasy feeling that something unseen walked beside her!

Students hurried past her, looking for their lockers and classrooms. Nora looked at the sheet she had received at orientation last night with her locker number. She looked at the row of lockers and walked along until she came to the one assigned to her.

She read the numbers of the combination and carefully followed the directions. Nothing happened. She tried again, but the locker wouldn't open.

"Having trouble?" asked a girl at the next locker.

Nora had been so absorbed in trying to open her own locker that she hadn't heard this girl come up.

"Yes," said Nora. "I've followed the instructions twice, but it won't open. I'm going to be late for class."

"Teachers are usually understanding the first day. Lots of kids have problems with their lockers. You'll get the hang of it," said the girl.

"Thanks," Nora said. "I hope it's soon! By the way, my name is Nora."

"Hi Nora! My name is Mia."

Just then the bell sounded for homeroom. Both girls rushed off.

"I'll see you later," called Nora.

Mia waved her hand and smiled.

Nora's homeroom teacher welcomed the class and asked if anyone had any problems. Nora and four other students raised their hands and told him about their locker problems.

"I'll help you after class," he offered.

Nora didn't take him up on his offer to help that morning. She decided to try again on her own after school. She didn't have too many things to carry around that day, so she really didn't need to use the locker between classes.

During every class, Nora looked for Mia. She hoped they would have a class or two together, at least. It would be nice to see a friendly face, but Mia was not in any of her classes.

Immediately after school, Nora went down the hall to her locker. Again she followed the directions carefully, but the locker would not open. Frustrated, Nora turned to go, but there stood Mia.

"I am surprised they assigned you that locker," she said. "They must have run short and had to use it."

"Why?" asked Nora. "What's wrong with this locker?"

"Ask your homeroom teacher to show you the security video of this hallway," said Mia. "You won't believe what's on it!"

"What *is* on it?" asked Nora.

"Something they caught on tape the night after the girl disappeared last year!" she exclaimed.

"What does that have to do with my locker?" asked Nora.

"What they caught on tape was a small ghostly figure that sailed in front of the camera, flew down the hall, and disappeared into this locker!" she said. "Some kids think the locker might be a portal."

"What's a portal?" asked Nora.

"It's an opening between this world and the next," explained Mia. "Something could be waiting in that locker and pull you right into the next world. Some kids think that's what happened to that girl who disappeared last year. They think that is her ghost caught on the security video."

"Oh, come on!" said Nora. "You're just trying to scare me because I'm new here. You made that up!"

"Ask around and you'll see I'm telling the truth," said Mia.

"I will," said Nora. "I'll ask my homeroom teacher in the morning."

"See you tomorrow," said Mia. "I have to go now."

At home that night after dinner, Nora told her mom and dad that she hadn't been able to open her locker yet. She also told them the story Mia had told her.

"I'm sure she was just teasing you," said her dad.

"If your teacher can't help you in the morning with the locker, I'll come over and see what I can do after school," said her mom.

"Is there such a thing as a portal?" Nora asked her parents.

"Some people say so, and there are some theories," her dad told her, "but I'm happy to say that I have never seen one, and I don't think there is any scientific research that validates portals. Now go finish your homework and get to bed."

Nora was eager to get to school the next morning. She was running late, though, and didn't have time to go to her locker. In homeroom, she raised her hand after attendance was checked and asked if she could ask the class something. The teacher gave her permission, and she asked the class about the girl's disappearance last year and if there was a security video with a ghost going into her locker.

She was surprised that the teacher and students were eager to talk about it.

"Let me show you the movie clip," said the teacher. "It will take just a minute to get it from the library."

He called the library, and a library aide quickly showed up with a DVD copy. It began with a shot of the empty hallway. Then suddenly, a white, ghostly figure flashed by the camera, flew down the hall, and disappeared into Nora's locker!

Nora was stunned. Apparently, Mia had told her the truth about the security video, but what about the portal? Surely there was no such thing as that.

"What does the disappearance of that girl last year have to do with this?" she asked.

"The Goodwin girl was last seen by her locker. It's your locker now. Her body was never found," said one of the students. "Some people think she was pulled into the next world when she opened her locker. Maybe her ghost haunts the school. Maybe that's her on the video."

The bell for first period interrupted the discussion, so Nora found out nothing else that day. After school, she decided to try one more time to open the locker.

Afternoon shadows had begun to fill the hallway. Nora approached her locker and put her backpack down on the hall floor. She was tired of carrying it home and back. She was tired of this nonsense about her locker. This time she was determined to keep trying the combination until she got it open. She looked at her directions and started to turn the lock. This time it seemed to turn itself. In fact, it opened without any difficulty at all. She pulled open the locker door and hesitated before looking inside. The shadows had deepened, and it was difficult for her to see clearly at first. Then her eyes focused on the back of the locker.

Something about it was not right. The back of her locker looked like it opened into the wall. She blinked and saw someone standing there. It was Mia! How did she get inside the locker?

This must be some kind of joke, she thought. *There must be some kind of door leading to a room or another hallway!*

"What's going on?" she asked. "This isn't funny! What are you doing here?"

"I'm Mia Goodwin, Nora! I'm here to take you to the other side."

Nora resisted, but Mia was very strong. Nora screamed as she was pulled through the back of the locker into the world beyond! Her screams reached a deserted hallway that was completely filled with shadows now.

When Nora didn't come home, her parents called the school and then the police. An extensive search over the next several months turned up nothing. There was no evidence of any foul play and no clues about her disappearance.

When the search was discontinued, the homeroom students asked the teacher if they could see the tape again. He requested a copy from the library, but as soon as the DVD started, they all felt something was wrong. The image had somehow been altered. It started out showing the empty hallway, but this time not one, but two ghostly figures flew by the camera, down the hall, and right into Nora's locker.

The homeroom teacher vowed silently to make sure that this particular locker would be taken out of use immediately. No other student should ever open that locker again!

The Stick Man

DeShawn, Luis, and Chad didn't know that you sometimes get what you wish for, and that sometimes you wish with your whole being that your first wish had not come true.

School had been in session for five weeks, and already everything had settled into a dull routine. On this particular warm September day, the three boys sat in Mr. Bennett's social studies class trying to think of something to break the monotony of reading an article about the production of bananas in South America.

They always had to answer a set of questions that Mr. Bennett passed out after he had given them time to finish reading. The class discussed the answers to his questions the next day. The routine had never varied. Read, answer questions, and discuss answers. Day after day after day! And then the boys experienced what they classified as a miracle. Mr. Bennett stood up behind his desk and rapped on it for attention.

"Class, I have an announcement that I think will be of interest to you. Since the warm September weather is continuing, my associate, Mrs. Ramirez, and I have decided to take our social studies classes on a three-day camping trip in Wyatt's Woods. Our purpose is to show you some of the early methods of surviving as pioneers. I am passing out a form for you to give to your parents, which they will need to sign in order to give permission for you to go. The forms contain a full explanation of our plans and procedures."

The boys were amazed! They tried picturing Mr. Bennett surviving in the woods! Mrs. Ramirez? Oh, yes! She could do it easily, but all three boys, and most of the class, considered Mr. Bennett a wimp.

Talk of the coming camping trip dominated all the students' conversations after school. Almost every student brought back the signed permission slip the next morning. A few parents expressed some concern about proper supervision, but Mrs. Ramirez assured them that some parents had volunteered to go along.

Mr. Bennett made another announcement at the beginning of class.

"Mrs. Ramirez has prepared our assignment for today," he informed them. "She felt that we should explore some of the local legends while we are camping in Wyatt's Woods, so she has made copies of the legend of the stick man, once believed to live by the pond deep in the woods. Read it and we will skip the questions and discuss it right now."

For once, the students read without sighing or complaining. None of them had ever heard of the stick man before.

The article described a stick man which had been sighted walking along the edge of the woods like a real human being.

Those who had spotted the strange figure felt sinister overtones to the encounters.

Two children headed to the pond to fish were chased away when the figure saw them. And a young couple that had gone hiking in the woods saw the stick man coming toward them, pointing its thin arms. They ran to their car, but incredibly, the stick man followed at superhuman speed. They raced from their car to their apartment complex door, ran down the hall, but barely made it inside before the stick man was tapping on the door. The young couple covered the keyhole with duct tape and stuffed towels under the door, holding them in place, but the stick man seemed intent on getting to them. He tapped, tapped all around the door and finally gave up and tapped his way down the hall.

The legend gives no explanation for the stick man's existence, but some people believe that the stick man is the angry spirit of the forest that won't accept the destruction of trees and wildlife by thoughtless humans.

"This story is a bunch of garbage," DeShawn said, pitching the article down on his desk. "There's no such thing as a stick man! It couldn't walk around without a brain or eyes or a body."

"Right!" agreed Chad. "If there is such a thing, I'd like to meet up with it!"

"So would I!" said DeShawn. "I wish we could meet up with a stick man!"

"Me, too!" exclaimed Luis. "Bring it on!"

The class laughed! The bell rang, dismissing school, and the students went home to prepare for the camping trip.

Two bright yellow school buses were parked in front of the school when the students arrived. Mrs. Ramirez directed the girls to the bus she was riding, and Mr. Bennett directed the boys to the other bus where he was in charge. The parents who had volunteered followed the buses in their own cars.

The Wyatt's Woods campsites were not too far away, so the group soon reached their destination and unloaded the gear. The students were so excited about the new surroundings that they barely noticed the two school buses driving away. They were away from school and ready for adventure!

It was nearing lunchtime, so Mr. Bennett handed out the sack lunches the school cafeteria had prepared. The students downed the food quickly because they wanted to get on with the day's activities.

"Let's get the tents set up first," said Mrs. Ramirez, taking charge while Mr. Bennett stood looking around bewildered. "Who has had any camping experience?"

Several students stepped forward. In a matter of minutes, Mrs. Ramirez had the work organized, with the experienced campers helping the inexperienced ones.

Chad, DeShawn, and Luis were permitted to share a tent at their parents' requests. Several other friends had been grouped together, too. Soon the tents were up, and the students gathered to hear more instructions from Mrs. Ramirez.

"Listen up," she told the group. "I do not want anybody wandering off from the groups. Is that clear?"

"Yes, Mrs. Ramirez," they answered.

"We will now divide into groups and gather wood for the campfire," she instructed. "There will be an adult assigned to each group, and you are to obey that adult without question. You are all to stay away from the pond. We don't know anything about it yet, so it's off limits for today. I don't want one of you to drown! Do you understand?"

"Yes, Mrs. Ramirez," they answered again.

DeShawn, Chad, and Luis knew they were going to explore that area around the pond sometime during this camping trip. They would stay alert for a good time. DeShawn noticed that one of the volunteer fathers came along with their group, even though Mr. Bennett was the leader. Mrs. Ramirez had likely sent him along on purpose. It turned out that this was a good thing, because about half an hour into the wood gathering, they all realized they were lost. The forbidden pond, dark and murky in the early afternoon shadows, lay right in front of them!

The three boys looked at each other with the hint of a smile.

"Oh, my," said Mr. Bennett. "I guess we took the wrong trail."

He gave a very distressed glance to the volunteer father.

"That's easy for anybody to do," the volunteer father said tactfully. "I think this is the trail back."

The group turned and followed the volunteer father back toward camp. Chad, DeShawn, and Luis looked at each other and looked at the pond. A chill crept over them. Something was unnatural about this place. They could feel it, and it scared them just a little bit.

None of the three boys had seen enough of the pond, though, so they took careful note of how the trail wound through the woods in case they should decide to go back to the pond again. The boys thought about the eerie silence of the pond itself, but they were sure they heard a faint tapping sound among the trees along the bank. All three boys had the feeling that something was watching them, and they were relieved when their group reached the campsite.

The volunteer parents lost no time in starting the campfire and helping prepare supper for the campers. Hot dogs and chips tasted especially good outside. The s'mores added to the complete success of their first meal prepared by the campfire. After the meal was over, Mrs. Ramirez addressed the group gathered around the fire.

"Did anyone see any evidence of the stick man this afternoon?" she asked, smiling.

The campers remembered the legend they'd read and noticed for the first time that shadows had moved around their circle. Most of them shivered, and they all moved a little closer together.

"Thank goodness he didn't show himself to us," said Mr. Bennett. "I'm afraid we ended up at the pond by mistake, but nothing happened to support the local legend."

Something cracked like a stick just beyond the circle as he finished speaking.

The campers jumped, and Mr. Bennett turned very pale. Suddenly the legend didn't seem so much like garbage as possible reality! Off in the woods, a faint tapping sounded, and the campers glanced over their shoulders. Chad, Luis, and DeShawn gave each other a very slight nod.

"Why do you think this spirit would be so angry, if there is really something to this legend?" asked Mrs. Ramirez.

"Mankind destroys the woods without giving anything back," suggested one girl.

"Very good," replied Mrs. Ramirez. "Does anyone else have any ideas?"

More responses came from around the circle about environmental values, and by the time they had finished, most of the campers were shivering at the thought of the stick man that might be out there in the woods. Nobody protested when Mr. Bennett announced bedtime, and they all snuggled down in their sleeping bags as far as they could get.

Inside their tent, Luis, DeShawn, and Chad lay in their sleeping bags waiting for the others to go to sleep. Without the need to discuss it, they knew they were going to sneak down to the pond that night. At last, their wish to see a stick man might come true!

Finally, the campsite was quiet, and the three boys silently slipped out and made their way along the trail to the pond. They didn't speak until they were standing on the bank. Gradually, a fog formed over the pond, and all the night sounds stopped.

"We shouldn't be here," said DeShawn. "This is a magic place or a sacred place or something."

Tap! Tap!

"What was that?" whispered Luis.

"The wind is blowing a branch against something," said Chad.

"That's stupid! There's no wind tonight!" said DeShawn.

Tap! Tap!

It was louder and closer now.

"I think we had better get out of here," said DeShawn.

Luis and Chad nodded in agreement.

The three almost fell over each other as they ran down the path toward camp. They slowed down about halfway to catch their breath.

"Just look at us," said Chad. "Running like scared rabbits! What if the others saw us running away like that? We'd never live it down."

"You're right," said Luis.

"Yeah," said DeShawn. "We've got to go back and check it out."

The boys walked silently back to the pond. They stood listening, but no sound came to them. The fog seemed to know they were there.

DeShawn broke the silence.

"Okay, we came back. I still think we shouldn't disturb this place. We should get out of here."

Before they could put his suggestion into action, a figure emerged from the fog around the lake. It had arms and legs and a body of sticks. They stood frozen in their tracks. They wondered how it could move without anything to give it orders, but it had a power of its own. It was suddenly right in front of them, and fear broke their paralysis.

"Run!" screamed DeShawn. "Run as fast as you can!"

They ran, but it was close behind them. Each boy realized that the thing they had wished for had materialized, and every instinct told them it had come for human lives. Each boy wished the first wish could be taken back, but they knew in their hearts that would not happen. They could only hope to outrun the evil stick man.

Tap! Tap! Scratch!

Chad felt a stick scrape his back!

Tap! Tap! Scratch!

Luis felt a scratch on his throat.

Tap! Tap! Scratch!

DeShawn felt a searing pain as a stick ripped down his leg! Somehow they kept running, but the mindless stick man stayed right on their heels. There was no stopping him from carrying out the mission he was determined to accomplish. They stumbled into the camp to give a warning, but it was too late. He was with them.

Tap! Tap! Tap!

The sleeping campers awoke and sat up, but sticks were flying through the air everywhere!

Tap! Tap! Rip!

The sleeping bags were ripped open. The campers felt themselves changing, growing hard and wooden like the other sticks flying in the air.

Tap! Tap! Scratch! Scratch! Crack! Crack! Crack!

Shattering screams mixed in.

The frenzy finally subsided. Nothing moved. The full moon looked down and shone on a site that looked forever unoccupied.

When the school officials did not hear from the teachers, they sent the police to check and see if they were all right. The campers were gone without a trace. The cars of the parent volunteers sat undisturbed, but no living, human thing could be found.

The police closed the woods and the campground while search parties were sent out. Day after day, they searched but found no clues.

The police chief looked at the exhausted volunteer searchers and rescue workers.

"We've done everything humanly possible," he said. "We'll take one more look tomorrow and call off the search."

The next day, they made one more sweep of the area and then called off the official search. They found no evidence that anyone had ever been in Wyatt's Woods. They stood by the pond, listening to a soft sound coming from the trees along the bank.

Tap! Tap! Tap!

"There's nothing here," said the police chief. "Let's open the campsite again to visitors."

They stood there looking around before they left the woods. All they saw was a huge pile of sticks by the campsite. They decided to leave them for other campers to burn in their campfires.

The Withered Hand

Coach Cameron Hart sat in his office off the gym at the high school where he had worked for the past five years. He left the door open to alleviate the feeling of being closed in. He couldn't bear that feeling now. September leaves were beginning to display their colors, and students and teachers were back in their classrooms like nothing horrible had happened during those recent summer days. And yet, leaving the door open was like opening himself to the summer tragedy instead of shutting it out. Life should be good right now. He was going to get a big raise soon, and he was going to be able to afford the new car he wanted. He should not be shrouded in guilt.

It had definitely been his fault, but so far, nobody knew that but him and the boy, Aaron Jones, and neither of them were talking. All Coach Hart had to do was keep his mouth shut, and his job with a fat new raise would be safe. Aaron couldn't tell anybody, but a little voice in Coach Hart's head whispered over and over, "Why not?" He got so frustrated that he almost yelled, "Because he's dead! That's why not!!!"

Aaron Jones had been one of his best football players. Aaron, along with Coach Hart's favorite player, Zac Harris, had been competing for a scholarship to college in the fall. The scout was due to come to the game just before Aaron's accident. Aaron had looked forward to this opportunity. He spoke of little else. Coach Hart thought Zac was more deserving. Zac's attitude and team spirit were much better than Aaron's. Coach Hart wouldn't have much input in the decision, but he would swing it in Zac's favor if he had the opportunity.

He remembered the day that changed everything. The team had been practicing for a couple of hours in the burning August sun when Aaron called time out for a water break.

"Coach," he said, "I need to take a break. My head hurts, and I'm getting a little dizzy out there in the sun."

"Aaron, the team doctor cleared you to play," Coach Hart reminded him. "Now get back in the scrimmage!"

"But Coach, I feel pressure at the top of my head all the time," Aaron insisted. "Now I'm dizzy. If I don't take care of myself, I won't do my best when that scout comes."

So that's it, thought Coach Hart. *He's wimping out of practice to save himself for the game.*

That realization really irked Coach Hart. Zac would never do that.

"You want time out?" he asked. "What makes you so special? Do you see Zac asking for time out? He pulled a muscle in his shoulder two days ago, but do you hear him complaining? No! He's out there doing his best!"

"But Coach Hart," Aaron protested, "a shoulder injury's just not the same!"

"Don't talk back to me, kid!" he yelled. "Get back on the field or I'll kick you off the team!"

"But coach, I didn't do anything. You can't throw me off the team," said Aaron.

Coach Hart was really angry now. Aaron always had an attitude. Zac always cooperated without a word. Aaron needed a lesson.

"Do you want to see if I can kick you off the team, Aaron?" he asked, glaring at Aaron. Coach Hart couldn't help it. He simply never liked this kid!

"No, sir," said Aaron. "I'll play."

Aaron walked back onto the field, and the team continued practice. About ten minutes passed before it happened. It was so fast that Coach Hart wasn't sure what took place. Aaron was tackled hard and went down. Several other players ran by, blocking Coach Hart's view for a few seconds. Then he clearly saw Zac's foot stomping down hard on Aaron's right hand, grinding it into the field and crunching the bones.

There was no doubt about it. Zac had intentionally injured Aaron! Zac would be disqualified and suspended from school if that action were exposed. There could possibly be criminal charges. Zac had made certain Aaron would not play in front of the scout and probably would never play anywhere again.

Coach Hart had to decide then and there what he was going to do, and his dislike for Aaron made his decision. It was an accident as far as he was concerned. In fact, unless somebody else saw Zac do it, he wouldn't say anything about it at all.

"Coach Hart! Come quick! Aaron's hurt!" one of the boys shouted.

Practice ended with the shouting. Coach Hart ran to the field behind the trainer and knelt beside Aaron. It was clear that he was not conscious.

"Quick," he ordered. "Call 911!"

Events moved quickly. The EMS arrived, and Aaron's parents were called. Coach Hart followed the ambulance to the hospital and met Aaron's father and mother in the ER.

"I told Aaron to tell you about the pressure in his head," Aaron's father told Coach Hart. "I told him to tell you if he got too hot or anything. Did he talk to you about it?"

"No," he lied. "I wouldn't have let him practice if I had known he was sick."

Coach Hart waited with Aaron's parents during the surgery.

"Why did it have to be his right hand?" his mother asked. "He won't be able to play football with a crippled, withered hand, and that's his whole life!"

"He was counting on that scholarship," said his dad. "We don't have the money to send him to college."

Coach Hart just nodded. He didn't know what to say. Finally, the doctor came and told them the surgery was over.

"He's awake now," said the doctor, "if you would like to see him. He asked about his hand. I've told him that we can do reconstructive surgery later, but his hand will never be quite the same. I don't think he is taking it well. Maybe you can talk to him."

"Did he hurt his head again?" asked his mom.

"I am a little worried about that," said the doctor. "All we can do at this point is wait and see. You can go on in now."

"You can come, too, Coach Hart, if you'd like to. He thinks so much of you!" said Mr. Jones.

Coach Hart couldn't think of any reason not to go, so he followed along behind them. The doctor came in last.

The coach was sorry about the incident, but he was thinking now about his responsibility in this whole thing. He would be in serious trouble if anybody learned that he had ordered Aaron to play when he was dizzy.

Will he tell anyone what I did? Coach Hart wondered.

The parents and coach stood by the bed. Aaron did not look like a football hero, lying there in those sterile hospital surroundings.

"You'll be all right, son," his mom said to him. "Doctors can do great things these days."

"Your mom is right," his dad told him. "You'll soon be back to your old self!"

Aaron's face turned furious. He looked straight into Coach Hart's eyes. The coach had never seen such a mixture of anger and despair and hatred!

"You know they're wrong, don't you, Coach? You know I'll never play ball again! My life is over and you know it! Tell them!"

"Aaron," said the doctor. "Calm down! We haven't determined the extent of your injury yet."

Aaron suddenly fell back on his pillow. He put his good hand to his head, gave one loud cry, and was silent.

"Aaron ...." the coach said but never got to finish.

The doctor interrupted.

"I need to check him," said the doctor. "You need to wait outside!"

They had been outside only a moment when a call came for the head trauma team to report to Aaron's room stat!

After the trauma team's arrival, it was only a few minutes before the doctor came out shaking his head.

Aaron Jones had died of a head injury, just like that. The blow to his head today must have impacted his previous injury.

The coach went to the funeral, but all through the service he felt like Aaron was not in that coffin! He felt him above, staring down at him.

"Get a grip!" he told himself. "Aaron didn't tell anyone before he died, and he sure can't tell now!"

The last few days had made the coach question that, though.

School had started, and Coach Hart received his raise. He had gone out right away and purchased the sporty new car he wanted, and he tried to put Aaron out of his mind. Zac Harris was offered a full scholarship. Life seemed to be going the way Coach Hart had dreamed. Only one thing marred his more prosperous lifestyle now.

There were signs that Aaron Jones was not resting in his grave! Of course, Coach Hart would never say he believed a thing like that, but there were signs he couldn't ignore.

Each day as he gazed at his open office door, he had experienced the same thing. A football had hit the floor in the hallway and rolled into his office. After a couple of days, he didn't need to get up and look outside. He knew that there wouldn't be anyone there—at least no one he could see. He didn't have to see the boy. He knew it was Aaron Jones, and he knew what Aaron wanted: revenge!

Coach Hart tried closing the door, but the football would be outside. Then he began to avoid his office altogether. He mostly conducted all his business from his new car!

The days passed. Coach Hart began to relax and enjoy a winning football season. Some close friends decided to honor him with a dinner at the country club outside of town. Clouds were rolling in as he headed his sleek, new car toward the country club, but even the cold rain that began to fall could not dampen his spirits.

As Coach Hart approached a sharp curve about a mile from the restaurant, his car suddenly became very cold. It shot forward as a heavy weight pressed on his foot! A tree loomed ahead in the curve. He tried to reach the brakes, but his feet wouldn't budge. Coach Hart tried to turn into the curve, away from the tree, but something covered his hand and steered the car toward the tree. Right before the impact, Coach Hart caught a glimpse of a withered hand covering his hand on the wheel as it guided the car into the tree.

The explosion could be heard as far away as the country club! Flames erupted into the rainy night. Emergency vehicles raced down the slick road. Coach Hart didn't have to worry, though. Accidents no longer concerned him. Aaron Jones chuckled as he welcomed his old coach onto a new playing field!

The Field Trip

When Peter Lim became a teacher, he didn't realize how many jobs he would have to do outside his classroom. This early morning bus duty was one of them.

He took a sip of hot coffee from his travel mug, pulled his coat tighter, and tried to make out the numbers on the school buses as they pulled in by the gym to drop off students. He read number 2029, number 2030, and number 2213. Then he saw bus number 2013 unload a group of students and then pull up to the cafeteria doors to pick up Mrs. Noor's class for a field trip.

That's odd, he thought. *I don't recognize any of those students who just got off. I guess the morning mist is affecting my vision.*

The students looked straight ahead and didn't speak, except for one little boy.

"Hi," he said. "You must be new here."

"Yes, I am," he said. "I'm Mr. Lim, the language arts teacher."

"I'm Mason Sawyer," he said. "I've got to go inside. I don't like this mist."

"Bye, Mason," said Peter.

He agreed completely. He didn't like the mist either.

Conley Elementary School was by the river, so morning mists were not unusual. Today, however, this mist was extremely thick and cold. The light from the cafeteria windows could not penetrate it more than a few feet.

There was an unusual chill about the mist this morning. Peter felt he was actually part of the mist. He would be glad when he could go back inside to his classroom.

This was Peter's first year teaching. He had been so excited when he first held his teacher's certificate in his hands. What a difference he could make with this opportunity! He had so many creative plans in mind already.

The first nine weeks hadn't been what Peter expected, but he hadn't given up on his ideals. Surely the endless paperwork, the countless e-mails to and from parents, and the daily meetings with the principal and faculty would end soon, or at least taper off.

Peter taught language arts, and he could have used this morning to complete his reviews of his students' papers, but he knew that Mrs. Noor's class trip to the Science Museum was important, too. He had heard a few odd comments, though, from some of the other teachers.

"It's been ten years ago today," said the art teacher.

"I wonder if she realizes that," said the counselor.

"What are you talking about?" Peter asked.

"Ten years ago, there was a deadly bus crash," said the counselor. "A busload of Conley students crashed, and all of the students were killed."

"Oh, no! What happened?" asked Peter.

"It was a head-on collision on the interstate," said the art teacher, Mr. Wills.

"It was a misty morning like this," the counselor continued. "A truck came from out of the mist on the wrong side of the road, and the school bus had nowhere to go. It happened too fast."

"I lived in another city ten years ago," said Peter. "I never heard about it."

"It's too painful for some people to talk about, so we don't discuss it very often," said the counselor.

The conversation was ended by the rush of morning activities, and Peter put the crash out of his mind.

The first bell sounded.

Only ten more minutes to go, he thought. *Then I can head for my nice warm classroom!*

Peter looked around. All the buses seemed to have come and gone. Number 2013 was parked and waiting for the field trip students by the cafeteria door.

Peter saw Mrs. Noor's class file into the cafeteria and take seats at the tables. He watched Mrs. Noor take attendance and collect the permission slips, then check to see if all the students had their lunch bags.

"Wait here quietly," said Mrs. Noor. "I need to give the attendance report and the permission slips to the office. I'll be right back."

The children remained seated. Then Peter saw the bus driver come to the bus door and motion for the kids to board.

"That's odd," Peter said to himself. "They should have waited for Mrs. Noor."

He walked over toward the bus, but since the children were being seated in a very orderly manner, he saw no reason to interfere. The driver closed the door just as Mrs. Noor came running out of the cafeteria. Nobody noticed the little boy who walked out behind her.

"Where's my class?" asked Mrs. Noor.

"They all got on the bus," said Peter.

"What!" exclaimed Mrs. Noor. "They were supposed to wait for me!"

At that moment, bus 2031 pulled up. The driver opened the door.

"Hey," he called out. "This is the bus for the field trip. What's going on?"

"They took our place on the bus," a small voice said. "Now we're free."

Peter looked down. There stood Mason Sawyer. Mrs. Noor noticed him for the first time!

"It can't be you, Mason!" gasped Mrs. Noor. "You died ten years ago!"

Bus number 2013, with the children aboard, pulled away from where it had been parked by the cafeteria.

"Stop that bus!" Peter shouted.

The counselor looked at Mason Sawyer, turned deathly pale, and fainted.

The driver of bus 2031 that was supposed to take the children to the Science Museum radioed for help.

Peter and Mrs. Noor stood helplessly watching as the taillights of bus 2013 disappeared into the white misty morning.

The Bully Man

Third Street Middle School loomed like a massive monster waiting for a meal. It was the beginning of the fall term, and students would soon be consumed by classes, homework, and after-school activities.

Kamal Tahir was glad that Natalie Wingate was his next-door neighbor and had already attended Third Street Middle School last year in the sixth grade. He had been worried when his family had moved to a different city, but it would be easier entering the seventh grade with a new friend who already knew her way around.

"I hope we get the same classes," said Kamal.

"We probably will," said Natalie. "They usually make out class schedules alphabetically. Our last names start with letters near the end of the alphabet, so they'll put us together. We'll probably have the same homeroom, too."

"Who are the best teachers?" asked Kamal.

"They are all okay, except Mr. Pippens," said Natalie. "If
you get him, transfer out if you can. He doesn't give you the
grade you earn; he grades according to how much he likes you."

"Then I would have it made!" laughed Kamal. "Everyone
loves me!"

"Oh, yeah!" replied Natalie, laughing too. "Come on, Mr.
Charm! We don't want to be late. Mr. Bully Man will get us!"

"You mean the Boogie Man?" asked Kamal.

"No, I mean Mr. Seaton, our principal," Natalie explained. "We call him Mr. Bully Man!"

"Why?" asked Kamal. "Is he that bad?"

"Worse!" said Natalie. "He thinks he's something big! He
enjoys picking on everybody."

They saw him at the other end of the hallway, so they
hurried to the gym to get their class assignments. They com-
pared schedules as they left to go to their homerooms.

"Great!" said Kamal. "We're in the same classes."

"Yeah," said Natalie. "We can do our homework together."

The first day went smoothly for Kamal and Natalie. They
saw Mr. Bully Man chewing out some kids for being late to
class, but they hurried in the opposite direction.

They were not so lucky as the days passed. Mr. Bully Man
had encountered them several times engaged in behavior that
did not please him. They were late to class once, dropped papers in the hall, talked in the library, and did other similar
things that Mr. Ronald Seaton, Bully Man Extraordinaire, considered offensive. He made it a daily ritual to find some reason
to pick on and punish the two friends.

Finally, Kamal and Natalie had endured enough! They
had to think of something to do to get revenge on the Bully

Man! They discussed it on their way home from school one afternoon.

"What are we going to do about him?" asked Kamal.

"I don't know, but we have got to do something soon to get him off our backs," said Natalie.

"Do you think it would do any good if we told our parents about how he picks on us?" asked Kamal.

"No, that would make it worse," said Natalie. "He would really be out to get us then."

"Then what are we going to do?" asked Kamal. "I hate going to school, because of him."

The friends had reached their homes, so the conversation had to end.

"Come over after dinner tonight," said Natalie. "Tell your folks we're doing homework, but we'll decide on a plan to pay Bully Man back!"

"Good idea," said Kamal. "I'll see you then."

To both Natalie and Kamal, dinner seemed to take forever. Finally, it was over, and Kamal told his parents that he and Natalie needed to do some homework together. They were pleased that the friends were so serious about their homework, so they gave Kamal permission to go.

The Wingates were equally pleased to see the friends display such an interest in school, so they left them alone in Natalie's room to work.

As soon as they were alone, Kamal said, "Did you come up with any ideas?"

"We can't do something silly like put a tack on his seat," said Natalie.

"We need to find something that he's afraid of," said Kamal.

"That's it!" said Natalie. "You're right! We have got to find out what he's afraid of and use it against him!"

"How can we find out?" asked Kamal.

"We're in his office for punishment enough to pick up information," said Natalie. "The next time we're in there, we'll keep our ears open."

"Agreed!" said Kamal.

They finished their homework quickly, and Kamal went back home happy that they had a plan.

They had an opportunity to put their plan in action the next day. The friends were running in the hall to get to class on time. Bully Man started ranting at them right there.

"I've a good mind to take you two to my office and put you in detention!" he shouted.

Kamal cringed, but Natalie spoke up and told him, "My mom said I can't be kept after school."

"Oh, she did, did she?" sneered Bully Man. "We'll see about that. You get to class, Kamal Tahir. You come with me, Natalie Wingate. I'll teach you not to sass me, girl!"

Kamal hurried to class, and Bully Man took Natalie into his office. Kamal was sorry that his friend was getting punished, but he had the feeling that Natalie provoked Bully Man on purpose.

A few minutes passed, and Natalie returned to class. She winked at Kamal as she took her seat. Kamal could hardly wait until class was over. They walked out together, and Natalie pulled Kamal aside.

"I've got some helpful information," she said. "It is well worth the punishment."

"What is it?" asked Kamal. "What did you find out?"

"Well, the big ole Bully Man is afraid of crickets!"

"Crickets!" exclaimed Kamal. "How do you know?"

"He had me sit and wait," said Natalie. "I overheard his assistant call an exterminator to get rid of a cricket in his office that had been driving him nuts. The assistant even laughed when he told pest control that his boss was afraid of crickets."

"That's so funny!" said Kamal, laughing. "A grown man afraid of a cricket!"

"Well, now that we have this information, what are we going to do with it?" asked Natalie.

"We could tell everybody at school, and they would laugh at him," suggested Kamal.

"I think most kids are too scared of him to laugh," said Natalie. "Besides, they might think we just made it up because he picks on us."

"We could catch several crickets and put them in his desk drawer," said Kamal.

"Hey," said Natalie. "That's not a bad idea. When he sees them, he will go off the deep end, and the kids can see his reaction! They'll know we didn't make it up!"

"Where do we catch crickets around here?" asked Kamal.

"I don't know," said Natalie. "Where do crickets live?"

"I think I heard one in our basement," said Kamal. "They are in all sorts of places, though. We could look by the river, in fields and bushes, under leaves or cardboard. We could even put out cricket food."

"We'll have to catch them," said Natalie. "I'm not spending my money on cricket food."

"Me, either," said Kamal.

"How do we catch them?" asked Natalie. "Do we sneak up and grab one when we hear it chirping?"

"Nope, they are too hard to catch with your hands," said Kamal. "We can try, though. And we can try putting a glass jar over them. I heard that you can put down a piece of cardboard outside and they will be under it in the morning."

For the next few days, the friends tried every place and every method that they could think of to catch crickets. They caught one huge cricket down by the river and others in various places. Finally, they had enough to put their plan into action.

"Maybe we shouldn't keep that big cricket," said Natalie. "We caught him by the river, and you know that chemical plant is accused of dumping toxic waste into the water. Maybe that's why he's so big."

"I don't really think the city would let them dump anything dangerous in the river," said Kamal. "I think we should keep him. We can put him in Bully Man's storage room and put the smaller crickets in his desk drawer. Now we just have to find a way to slip in."

"You keep the big one at your house," said Natalie. "There's something funny about that one."

Kamal agreed and put him in a container in the closet in his room. He was afraid the cricket would chirp and that his mom would discover it. It remained totally quiet, though.

Kamal checked on the cricket every hour, and he was beginning to worry. It looked like it was getting bigger every time he looked at it.

There was to be a football game after school the next day, so the school would be open. The two friends decided that that would be the perfect time to gain entrance without anyone being suspicious.

Kamal had to put the big cricket in a larger container. He didn't want Natalie to get a good look at it. She might insist that he let it go. He thought about it all day at school the next day. Everybody was excited about the game, so nobody paid attention to Kamal and Natalie as they slipped away.

They walked home after school and collected all their crickets. They snuck back to school and looked around to see if Bully Man was still around. His car was still there, so they looked to see if they could see him by the field. He was headed toward the school when they spotted him. They had enough time to put the crickets in his office before he could get there.

The friends were fast. Natalie dumped her crickets from their container into the desk drawer. Kamal put the huge cricket in the storage room, but didn't close the door completely. He wanted it to be able to get out.

They expected the crickets to chirp, but they didn't make a sound. The friends ran out of the office, out the side door, and hid behind some bushes near the office window. They saw Bully Man come in and sit at his desk. He followed his usual routine and opened his desk drawer for some papers. That's when the screaming started.

The friends ran from the bushes and peeked in the window. Bully Man was frantically flinging his arms, trying to fight off the crickets, but then he froze in terror. Natalie and Kamal could not believe what they were seeing.

The door to the storage room was wide open, and a cricket as big as a man was eyeing Bully Man. It gave one leap and was on him. Kamal and Natalie didn't stay to see the rest. It was too horrifying. Both friends ran to the bushes and were sick.

Bully Man's screams did not reach the ears of anyone except Kamal and Natalie because everyone else was yelling at the game. Nobody would check Bully Man's office until morning.

The friends did not look in the window again. They ran home as quickly as they could. Each one was thinking, *What have we done?*

If they had looked back or waited, they might have saved themselves. Maybe if they had gone for help, they might have been able to save themselves. But they didn't, so they didn't see what happened.

What was left of Bully Man was on the floor by his desk. The big cricket had a satisfied look on its face.

It jumped on Bully Man's chair. He saw *Ronald Seaton, Principal* on the nameplate. His chirp was almost a chuckle.

What a tasty fellow, he thought.

He hopped back into the storage room so he would not be discovered. He wouldn't leave until morning. Then he decided he would go to Kamal and Natalie's houses and eat them for breakfast.

Shadows in the Woods and by the Water

The Lake

Ava Goma slowed her car so she and her thirteen-year-old son, Wes, could get a good look at the lake. The wind rippled the surface like something big was swimming underneath. Something about the movement of the water did not bode well!

"Cool!" said Wes, who obviously did not share her foreboding.

What's wrong with me, she thought. *My imagination is getting the best of me. No unearthly thing that big could possibly exist in a small lake like this. There is nothing living in this lake but fish!*

She hadn't been up here since she was a child visiting her Aunt Trina, but she was remembering now that she'd had an uneasy feeling about the lake even then. Some vague story about a boy drowning in the lake came back to mind.

Low thunder drew her attention to the sky, and she saw a dark, billowing lake cloud moving in. Her foot automatically pushed down on the accelerator.

"Storms come up fast on the lake," she told Wes. "We need to get to the house and unload everything before this one hits."

Ava pulled the car into the driveway and was pleased to see that the lake house her aunt had left her in her will seemed to be in good condition, at least from the outside. The surrounding woods were dark and silent, and she shivered, feeling a bit uncomfortable about being so isolated. They were about ten miles from town, and the only other house she and Wes had seen was around the bend down the road. She had only glanced at it quickly, and it had looked deserted.

I'll have to check it out later, she thought. *Maybe there are some neighbors on down the road in the other direction.*

She was sad that Aunt Trina had died, but this inheritance had come at the best possible time. The apartment she and Wes shared was being turned into a condo that she couldn't afford to buy. Since her husband's death in a car accident last year, she had been able to make it on her earnings as a writer, but she hadn't qualified for a condo loan. This lake house was hers now, and it would be the perfect place to write. Wes loved the outdoors like his father, so he would have lots of places to explore.

The thunder rumbled, reminding her it was giving her a short break, but not for long. Since the house was completely furnished, Ava and Wes had only brought their clothes and boxes of personal items. She had purchased some groceries in town and bought McDonald's cheeseburgers, Cokes, and fries for their dinner. They quickly unloaded the car and carried the last boxes inside as the storm cloud became impatient and decided not to spare them any longer.

Ava was relieved that both the power and water compa-
nies had already activated their services as promised. Ava and
Wes both felt tired and hungry from their trip, so they gobbled
their McDonald's food as if it were a feast! Sounds from the
storm distracted them. The wind roared down the chimney,
and raindrops beat against the windowpanes as if they were
frightened living things desperate to break through the glass.
And then everything became still.

Suddenly the silence was broken by the sound of a shrill
scream down by the lake. Ava and Wes ran to the window, but
it was too dark to see anything. The storm started up again,
making it very dangerous for them to go outside and see if
someone needed assistance.

"Should we go see if someone needs help?" asked Wes.

"No," Ava told him. "We don't know our way around yet,
and the storm's too severe for us to go out in it, wandering
around alone in the dark."

"Should we call someone?" asked Wes.

"Our phone won't be turned on until tomorrow," she
told him.

"Try your cell phone," Wes suggested.

"I'm trying," she answered, "but I'm not getting a signal.
It must have been an animal of some kind. I don't think a person would be out in this storm."

"It didn't sound like an animal," Wes insisted. "It sounded
human."

"I don't hear anything now, so I think we'd better get to
bed," she said.

"Aw, Mom," said Wes, "we haven't even explored the
house yet. Where are we going to sleep?"

He does have a point, she thought. *I guess a quick look around wouldn't hurt.*

The house had three bedrooms, two of which overlooked the lake. Wes and Ava chose these as their bedrooms and soon were settled in for the night. Both tossed and turned, and sleep did not come easily.

Morning brought breakfast along with the feeling that the house, the woods, and even the lake were normal.

"Mom, is it okay if I fish off that dock at the lake?" asked Wes.

"It's okay if you promise not to wade in the lake or go swimming," she answered.

"I promise," he said. "You know I'm old enough to stay out of a strange lake!"

Wes took his fishing pole and some bait and sat down on the dock to fish all morning. Ava spent the morning unpacking and getting organized.

At noon, Wes came in carrying six fish he had caught for supper. The telephone company technician came, installed the phone, and turned on the service. Ava was surprised at how relieved she was to have a working phone.

"Does anyone live in the house around the bend?" she asked the technician as she was leaving.

"Not anymore," she replied. "They moved away after their little boy disappeared in the lake a few years ago."

"Disappeared?" Ava asked. "It seems like an odd word to use if the boy drowned."

"He must have drowned," the woman said, "but they never found his body. The lake has a bad reputation. Most people don't go near it. They claim to see and hear odd things. You and your son should be on guard."

"Thank you," she said. "We will be!"

She was going to warn Wes again to be careful before he went back to the dock, but he made no move to go. Instead, he went to his room and unpacked his things and put them away without being told. He was unusually quiet at dinner.

"Is something wrong?" Ava asked him.

"Something happened at the lake this morning when I was fishing," he told her.

"What?" she asked.

"I was sitting there, letting my feet dangle in the water, when this boy came out of nowhere and sat down on the bank near me. Mom, he was covered with scars," Wes told her. "I asked him if he lived around here, and he said he used to."

"Did he say anything else?" Ava wanted to know.

"I asked him then if we'd be at the same school next fall," Wes said. "He just said he doesn't go to school anymore. I guess he must be home schooled because of those scars. I tried to keep from looking at his scars, but he didn't seem to mind when I did. He said it was okay when I stared for a few seconds.

"'What happened? Were you burned?' I asked him. He just shook his head.

"'Not fire,' he said. 'Acid.'

"Acid? I thought. How could a kid about my age get exposed to so much acid?

"Before I could ask, a dark shadow moved toward us under the surface of the lake. He yelled at me to pull my feet up fast, and I did. At that point, the shadowy thing stopped. It disappeared right there in the middle of the lake, but the water went around like a whirlpool. When I looked around, the boy was gone."

"How strange!" Ava said. "Something must have cast a shadow on the water."

"This was something under the surface," Wes said. "It was very scary."

The next day, Ava and Wes went to the nearby town to do some shopping. Wes had no time to go fishing in the lake. By the next day, however, he had gotten over his scare, so he decided to fish again in the late afternoon. He wore only his swim trunks so he could get some sun. It wasn't long until he felt all hot and sweaty. He stood on the dock and looked at the cool water.

Surely, a quick dip to cool off can't hurt, he thought.

Wes saw the scarred boy appear on the bank, waving his arms furiously. Wes hesitated.

Ava was writing and had gotten involved in her story. The sun had almost gone down before she realized it. She saved her work and shut down her computer. She looked for Wes, but he was nowhere to be found in the house.

He's got to be fishing, she thought, and she went outside to look.

Just then, a scream tore through the late afternoon air! Ava had never heard anything like it! The setting sun seemed to have turned to blood. The trees in the woods bowed to the force of the wind, and a scarred boy ran from them directly toward Ava.

"Stop him! Stop him!" he shouted.

"What are you talking about?" she asked.

"He's going to swim. The lake monster will swallow him, and the stomach acid will eat him alive!"

"Why would you say a thing like that?" Ava demanded.

"Because it happened to me. I'm the boy who disappeared in the lake a few years ago. The lake monster ate me that night for dinner!"

Terror took charge of Ava's senses. She realized she was running toward the lake. It wasn't too late! She could see Wes standing on the dock! She had to save him!

"Don't jump!" she screamed. But she was too late after all.

Wes jumped off the edge of the dock and plunged into the water. She saw the water churn and the shadowy monster rise to the top. It opened its mouth and snapped it shut as Wes disappeared inside.

Ava stood in disbelief. Her body felt like stone. This couldn't be happening. Had what she saw been real? Her mind refused to process what her senses told her. Then she heard something that penetrated her mind. She broke into a hysterical, panicked laugh at the sound she heard. It couldn't be what she thought it was, but she recognized the sound that was coming from the lake! Anybody would recognize it! It sounded for all the world like a giant burp!

River Crow

Jay Kapoor, his daughter, Kala, and his nephew, Dev, barely made it inside before the rain raced across the river, drenching the old tree on the bank and their fishing cabin like a monsoon. Then, after a few minutes, the rain slacked off to a lighter but steady downpour.

"We just made it in time," Jay said to the kids.

"I guess it will rain all night," said Kala. "I'd hoped it wouldn't rain while we were here."

"I like the rain," said Dev. "I always liked to hear it falling on the roof at Nana's house."

"You won't like it here!" said Kala.

"Why not?" asked Dev.

"There's something strange about rainy nights here," Kala told him. "Like that boating accident we heard about on the radio driving in. The boat capsized before the storm came in. There was no obvious reason for it to turn upside down in the water, but over it went!"

"There are all kinds of reasons for it flipping over. Maybe it was an undercurrent, or maybe someone rocked the boat," said Dev.

"Hey, guys," Jay interrupted. "Let's get our stuff stowed away and have something to eat."

It didn't take long to stow what they had brought, and it wasn't long until Jay had heated the pre-cooked stew and cornbread that he had brought along. They sat down and dug in.

"CAW!" they suddenly heard from outside.

Dev ran to the window and looked out.

"Uncle Jay," he said, "there's the biggest crow I've ever seen sitting in that tree. I never saw one at night before. I'd like to see it up close."

"It's bad luck to see just one crow at a time!" said Kala. "The rain and the crow coming together means something bad is going to happen. This could be the night of the curse."

"What's she talking about, Uncle Jay?" Ben asked him. "Is she just making up something to scare me?"

"Tell him about the curse, Dad," said Kala. "Tell him I'm not lying."

A gust of wind drove a burst of rain against the window. After that, it calmed down again as quickly as it had come.

"CAW!" the crow repeated.

Dev looked out again, and a flash of lightning showed him that the crow was still in the same spot.

"Someone died in the river this night years ago!" said Kala. "Somebody else will, too! The crow is a sure sign!"

"Enough of that," said Jay, clearing the table. "Let's leave local legends until tomorrow morning."

"Please tell me, Uncle Jay!" Dev pleaded. "I want to know now!"

"All right," said Jay, "but you've got to promise not to wake me up all night every time you hear a little noise."

"We promise, Uncle Jay! Right, Kala?" Dev said.

"I promise," Kala answered, not very enthusiastically. "I won't wake him. I've heard the story before."

"I will tell you the story if you will get ready for bed while I wash up the bowls and spoons," said Jay. They agreed and hurried off to change into their pajamas.

Jay thought of Dev and Kala as he did the dishes. He had hoped this fishing trip would bring them closer together. Two years ago, Dev's parents had died in a plane crash. Dev had gone to live with Jay's mom, Nana Kapoor. Then a few weeks ago, Nana Kapoor had died suddenly of a heart attack. Once more, Dev had no place to go. Dev had no other relatives, and Jay had taken him in, but Kala hadn't relished the idea of her cousin becoming her new "brother." Maybe spending this time together would help.

The kids were ready and waiting by the time Jay dried the last dish. He sat down and poked the fire in the fireplace. Kala and Dev moved closer.

The wind moaned and the crow answered, "CAW!" This time it sounded angry.

"This story started a long time ago," Jay began. "At one time, a small cottage stood near that old tree on the river bank. A woman lived there with her beautiful daughter. The old woman was not a beautiful person, though—at least not inside. She was very selfish and afraid of being left alone, so she took every means to keep her daughter from having friends or meeting young people who might be interested in her.

"The old woman had a large crow as a pet. It sat on the tree branch outside the cottage and cawed to warn her if someone was coming. Most people thought both the crow and the old woman were creepy. Some even called the old woman a witch. All but one young man kept their distance.

"This young man met the beautiful girl at the country store a few times, and they had talked. The attraction between them was immediate. They fell in love, and they vowed they would marry if it were the last thing they ever did.

"What could that old witch really do to keep me away from him? the daughter wondered. *I'm tempted to march right up to her and tell her I am going to see him, and she can't do anything to stop me!*

"The young man tried to approach the cottage one night, but the crow cawed loudly, and the old woman came to the door. When she spotted him, she raised her arms into the air and shouted for him to get away. A wind suddenly began to whirl around him, and he found that he couldn't move toward the cottage. He could only move away!

"The crow had cawed a couple of other times when he had tried to visit, but the young man turned and hurried away before the old woman could see him.

"The couple met secretly away from the cottage and eventually decided they would elope. They planned to sneak away one night, so they discussed how they would put their plan in action. They waited impatiently for darkness to come.

"A cloud lay back in the west, and thunder warned them that rain would be coming soon. Certainly they would not let a simple storm stop them. They would run away as planned. They had a boat tied up by the bank near the old tree. He would tap on her window, and they would dash to the boat. They would be gone across the river before her mother knew what had happened.

"But sometimes even the most perfect plan does not work out. The storm that the couple had ignored came in full force to the middle of the river. Just as they reached the same position, the river swirled around and around in the wind, and the couple were flung from the boat.

"When their lifeless bodies were carried ashore, the old woman screeched in anger and despair! 'A curse on this river! There will be a death each year until enough souls are sacrificed to allow my daughter to walk this earth again! My faithful crow will caw to count each one.'

"It was said that the old woman was never seen again. But on nights like this, people say the crow is keeping count of souls that pass over. When he counts enough, the young woman will return."

Jay finished the story and saw that both kids were wide-eyed, even though Kala had heard the story before.

"Do you believe that's true, Uncle Jay?" asked Dev.

"I think it is only a story," Jay answered.

"Me, too, but I'd like to get a good look at that crow," said Dev.

"Don't even think about it," ordered Jay. "That river bank can be pretty slippery in the rain, so it's dangerous to be walking around out there, especially after it rains. You two go straight to bed and stay there, okay?"

"You won't catch me out there," said Kala.

Dev said nothing at all.

The three of them went to bed and listened to the steady beat of the rain on the roof. The kids shared a room, and Jay slept in the room on the opposite side of the house. The sound of the rain lulled Jay and Kala off to sleep.

Dev wasn't sleeping, though. He was restless. He sat up in bed and looked out the window. The lightning still flashed occasionally, and it allowed Dev to see that the crow was still sitting in the tree by the river.

It wouldn't hurt to go out for a quick look, he thought. *Uncle Jay and Kala will never know I'm gone.*

He looked out the window again, and this time, the crow seemed to be looking at him.

"Stay right there, Old Crow," he whispered. "I'm coming out. I'm not scared of you!"

Dev got quietly out of bed. He had unpacked his raincoat when they first got there, so he found it without making any noise. Slipping it on, he carefully opened the door and stepped out into the rainy night.

At first, the night was normal. The wind remained calm, and the rain remained steady. He had forgotten his boots, and as he walked, his shoes quickly became soaked and slippery.

Squish! Squish!

He ignored the sound and waded on through the water toward the tree. The crow sat silently watching the boy approach.

Squish! Squish!

Dev was under the tree now, but he couldn't get a clear view of the crow from where he stood.

I'll have to move toward the river a little to get a good look, he thought.

Squish! Squish! Squish!

It all happened at the same time. The slick soles of his shoes slid in the mud, and Dev reached for something to hold on to, but there was nothing in reach.

"CAW!" said the crow.

Dev splashed in the muddy river. He was sucked into the mud at the bottom. He struggled, but slowly he gave up. He felt an extraordinary peace as he became the final sacrifice.

Inside the cottage, Kala woke up.

"Dad," she called. "Dev's gone!"

Jay ran into the room, and together, he and Kala looked out the window. They watched the huge crow fly away, and then they saw the most beautiful young woman they had ever seen walking slowly along the bank of the river toward the house.

The Well

"Mom, there's an eye in the sink," Alex announced.

"What!" exclaimed her mother.

"It's looking at me from the drain," she continued.

Hailey Carter started toward the sink where her daughter was standing, and the drain gurgled loudly.

"It's gone now," said Alex, as her mother stopped by her side.

"I knew this place was too good to be true!" said Hailey. "Beach houses don't come this cheap."

The family—Hailey, Kevin, and their daughter, Alex—had rented this house as a vacation home for the summer. It seemed perfect, except for the fishy smell coming from one of two sinks in the kitchen when they arrived last night.

It's odd for a kitchen to have two sinks, Hailey thought. *It's strange that one works perfectly and the other is clogged. I guess we'll have to call a plumber.*

Hailey tried to use a plunger, but the dirty water would not go down. She finally gave up and called the plumber.

"The kitchen sink, huh?" the plumber asked, coming in the door.

"Yes," said Kevin. "How did you know?"

"I have had a lot of calls about that sink," he said. "I'll tell you right up front that I haven't had much luck unstopping it. Local legend says it's cursed."

"Cursed?" asked Alex. "What do you mean?"

"There's a tale about a little girl drowning in a well before your house was built," he said. "They never found her body. Most folks thought at the time that she was washed out to sea. Some say her spirit is caught in the well that your kitchen is built over."

He stopped and began to pull something from the pipes. Kevin, Hailey, and Alex watched as he cleaned out gobs of green, slimy seaweed.

"How did seaweed get in our water?" Hailey asked.

"It's salt water," he told the family. "The well I was talking about is under your kitchen beneath the clogged sink! It's odd how salt water is getting into the pipes from the well. There may be an opening where seawater can flow in. Maybe it will stay clear for a while now, but call me if it doesn't."

Hailey decided when she saw the slimy seaweed that she would use only the sink that had no problems. Since the plumbing in the other sink worked fine, the family set aside the problem for a while until they got the rest of the house in order.

Finally, everything was in its place, and everyone fell into bed exhausted! It was about 2:00 a.m. when a noise in the clogged kitchen sink woke them. They knew they had locked the doors and windows, so they couldn't imagine what was moving around down there. The sound was muffled. They strained to hear what it was. It sounded like something flopping on the floor.

"It's probably a noise from the clogged pipes," said Kevin. "I'll call the plumber again in the morning. We may have to ask the owners to fill the well in."

Another flopping sound came up from the kitchen. This time it was followed closely by a scream.

They heard footsteps running up the stairs, and Alex came bursting through the door.

"Alex, what's that noise?" Hailey asked. "Who's down there?"

"It's got one eye," exclaimed Alex. "It flopped out on the floor and looked at me!"

"What was it? And why were you downstairs in the kitchen?" asked Kevin.

"I thought I heard something. I was curious," said Alex. "The thing came out of the clogged sink. It had one eye and a huge claw."

Kevin went downstairs to investigate. As he entered the kitchen, a gurgling sound came from the clogged sink. Kevin turned on the light and looked around. There was nothing on the floor except a wet spot where Alex had probably spilled some water. He detected a faint fishy smell, however.

He turned the light off and went back upstairs.

"Did you see it?" asked Alex.

"I couldn't find anything. There was nothing there," he told her. "I think you must have had a bad dream because of the story that plumber told you. Let's all go back to bed and get some sleep."

"I didn't dream it," Alex insisted.

"If anything was there, it's gone now," Hailey told her daughter. "We all need to get some sleep."

When morning came, Alex was still uneasy. While her mom started breakfast, she peeked in the clogged sink. There was no eye watching her this morning. She suddenly felt the urge to go out on the beach.

"Mom," she said, "I'm going to run down to the beach and see if any shells washed up last night, okay?"

"Yes, but don't take long. I'll have pancakes ready soon!" Hailey answered.

Alex raced to the water. As she ran to the beach, she thought something was watching her. Something was waiting in the water!

She stopped and looked at the ocean. Something was swimming near the beach. She could see a form in the water. The form wanted her to wade in toward it. Its thoughts told her so. She tried to resist, but her feet moved on their own.

Suddenly one huge claw snagged her and pulled her under. She held her breath and tried to break loose, but it pulled her down into a cave by the shore. Its one eye looked at her as it pulled her into a well.

This is under my house, she thought. *This is under the clogged sink.*

Her head was above the water in the well now, and she could see the creature clearly. It began to change, and she realized she was changing, too!

"I've been changed into this evil creature for years!" said a little girl, emerging. "I could only be released when I found someone to replace me. I picked you!"

"No!" screamed Alex as she struggled. "Let me go!"

But it was too late. Her two eyes had merged into one, and she could see her two hands had become a huge claw! The rest of her body had been transformed into a tiny fish!

She struggled through the pipes and looked through the drain. Her mother had finished making breakfast.

"Kevin, go call Alex! Tell her to come on in," she called to her husband.

While Kevin walked on the beach to look for the daughter he'd never find, Hailey had the oddest feeling that something was watching her from the clogged drain in the kitchen!

"Mom, look, there's an eye in the sink," said Alex, but her words only came out as a quiet gurgle.

Red Fang

Charlie Sadler knew she had made a mistake in coming to the cabin early, but she didn't want to stay home alone after her parents left on vacation. Her friends would want to come over and party, and she didn't want to say no to them. She definitely didn't want to get in trouble with her parents, either.

Going on a cruise didn't appeal to her in the least, especially after she had gotten seasick on a deep sea fishing trip she'd taken with her family several years ago. Her parents had agreed that working for her uncle would definitely be better than feeling queasy for two weeks.

At seventeen, she was perfectly capable of staying home alone, but she didn't like how the neighbors watched her every move when she was all by herself. Her Uncle Eli's offer was the perfect solution for her to get away and have some time alone.

"I bought the old cabin by Damron's Creek," Uncle Eli told Charlie. "I've been up there a few times fishing when the Damron family was staying there for the summer. Their daughter Sophie invited some kids from her class to come for fishing or bonfires. When it came up for sale, I thought it would be a good investment."

"What do you say?" asked Uncle Eli. "I need someone to clean up the cabin and the fishing shack. I don't think the place has been taken care of since the Damrons took Sophie away. I know you like the outdoors, so I figured you would be perfect for the job."

Charlie thought so, too.

"Sure, Uncle Eli! I'm your girl. I'll take provisions and my fishing gear," said Charlie. "I'll fix up everything like you want."

"Good," said Uncle Eli. "I knew I could count on you. Here's your pay in advance! There is just one thing, though. It would be a good idea if you stayed inside the cabin after dark. Mr. Damron said there are lots of animals in those woods that could kill someone. Who knows what else is in or around that creek."

"Yeah, I guess you're right," said Charlie. "The cabin is isolated. And nobody ever said what happened to Sophie."

"That's true," said Uncle Eli. "Rumor has it that she saw something in the woods that scared her half to death. People said she was not the same after that. She went crazy! Some say she is ill. They whisked her away to some hospital, and they never used this place again. Now, it has become an urban legend. Pay no mind to it. Just go inside by dark to be sure nothing bothers you."

"Okay, Uncle Eli," said Charlie. "We have a deal."

"Do you need me to go over the driving directions with you again?" asked Uncle Eli.

Charlie shook her head. She knew how to get there.

Charlie left right after she saw her family off for their cruise. She had plenty of time to get to the cabin before dark.

For some reason, she didn't want to be on the road in those woods after nightfall. Clouds had moved in overnight, and the threat of storms looked more serious now that Charlie was on the road. When she turned onto the narrow road that ran along the banks of Damron's Creek, the wind began whipping the branches along the side of the road. A poem that her silly thirteen-year-old sister made up to annoy her about her upcoming time in the woods came to her mind.

> *What are the limbs*
> *Reaching out from the trees?*
> *What monster's breath*
> *Am I calling a breeze?*

Her sister had repeated it over and over and over!

Knock it off, she told herself silently. *Nothing is reaching for me, and the wind is not a monster's breath blowing on me!* Her kid sister could always get under her skin! *Little creep!*

She followed the bend in the road and saw the cabin ahead on the right and the old fishing shack nearby on the creek bank. Both the cabin and the fishing shack looked a bit sinister in the growing shadows.

She had arrived just in time to beat the storm. Thunder was rolling through the sky, getting closer and closer with each rumble. Charlie unloaded the car in several quick trips. She closed the cabin door behind her as lightning flashed and rain drummed on the roof.

Charlie began to get jittery. There were sounds beside the storm that she couldn't identify. She wished now that she had stayed home where she would have had all the necessary conveniences and all of her things surrounding her, instead of being alone in this remote cabin.

The cabin had no electricity, so Charlie unpacked two of several battery-operated lanterns she had remembered to bring from home. The light from the lanterns held back the shadows in the corners, so her spirits began to rise. She was not in high spirits for very long, though. Above the rain, she heard a moaning sound coming from the old fishing shack.

Charlie hurried to the window and looked out. Through the sheets of rain, the fishing shack looked like a monster looming over the creek. A red glow was coming from the windows, and Charlie realized that the moaning sound was coming from in there, too.

What's going on, she wondered. *Is the shack on fire? Was it struck by lightning? Surely not. I didn't hear any thunder.*

The moaning sounded again.

Is something in there that needs help? Maybe an animal got trapped in there, or maybe someone took shelter from the storm.

As Charlie stood debating whether she should go to the shack and check or not, she remembered her uncle's warning about being out of the cabin after dark. Suddenly the red glow vanished and the moaning stopped! She watched for a moment, but nothing else unusual happened. It was like nothing strange had happened at all. She was grateful for that. She didn't want to go out in this storm anyway.

She realized that the drive had left her tired and hungry, so she opened the cooler she had packed before she left. She wolfed down two sandwiches between gulps of a soft drink, pulled her sleeping bag around her, and went to sleep.

Sometime in the night, the storm moved on, but Charlie was too sound asleep to notice. She awoke to sunshine and normal sounds of the woods.

She ate a breakfast of doughnuts and milk that was still cold in the cooler. While she ate, she mentally planned her agenda for the day. First, she would sweep the cabin floor and straighten up a bit. Then she would unpack supplies, gather wood for the fireplace, and take a look inside the old shack.

The cabin looked cozy when she finished sweeping and straightening. She wanted to avoid going to the fishing shack, but she decided it would be good to take a look and get it over with.

Charlie reached the door and stood listening for sounds or movement inside. She heard nothing, so she pushed open the door and looked around before stepping inside. She didn't know exactly what she was looking for, but she would welcome anything that would explain the moaning and the red glow last night. There was no evidence that any living thing had been inside recently.

She saw something stacked along the back wall that pleased her very much. It was firewood, all dry and ready to use. Now she wouldn't have to gather wet wood from the woods! Faint musty, earthy smells filled the shack and clung to some of the wood. She carried several loads to the cabin to use in the fireplace, and she carried some down by the creek where she planned to build a fire and cook her supper, assuming, of course, that the fish would be biting.

Charlie spent the afternoon relaxing on the creek bank. By late afternoon, she had caught three fish that would easily be enough for her dinner. She started the small fire quickly with the dry wood, cleaned the fish, and cooked them the way her father had taught her to do when they were camping. She felt very self-reliant eating the meal she had provided for herself.

The sun set behind clouds that reminded Charlie of the storms from the night before. The first boom of thunder destroyed the peace of the afternoon. Charlie put out the fire, picked up her fishing pole, and went inside the cabin. The cabin felt damp, so she built a fire in the fireplace. She rolled her sleeping bag out on the floor in front of the fireplace, turned on one of the battery lanterns for extra light, and read as the storm approached.

Normally, Charlie was not afraid of storms, but being alone out here in the woods made her feel jittery.

BOOM! CRACK! WHOOSH!

Thunder jarred the cabin, lightning lit up the room, and a burst of wind flung rain against the windows! It was as if the storm were trying to enter the cabin. Charlie put her book down and went to the window.

There was a red glow in the fishing shack again. She heard moaning, but it could have been the wind. Somehow she knew it wasn't. The tree limbs whipped in the wind and seemed to be reaching for her! They motioned and beckoned, and she thought of her sister's silly poem and shivered. The red glow vanished, leaving the old fishing shack standing like a dark monster in the flashes of lightning.

She wanted answers to all of her questions about the fishing shack, but she couldn't bring herself to go out in the storm. Instead, she crawled into her sleeping bag and lay awake listening to the storm move on.

She slept late. She looked outside to see what damage the storm had done. She couldn't see that any limbs were down.

That surprised her considering the force of the wind. The old shack lost its menacing look in the light of day. She walked down, opened the door, and was met with an unpleasant odor. It was the distinct smell of something rotting. She looked closely at a stick of wood and saw something that looked like a fang mark!

That's the smell of something that's been dead for a while, she thought.

Her thoughts were interrupted by the sound of a car horn. She looked up to see Uncle Eli's car coming down the road.

Uncle Eli jumped out of his car holding a large paper bag.

"Hey! How about some breakfast?" he called.

Charlie was happy to join him. Sausage, eggs, and biscuits had never tasted so good.

"What are you doing here?" asked Charlie.

"I wanted to make sure you were settled in and that you were okay after the storms the last two nights," said Uncle Eli.

"The storms didn't scare me; the fishing shack did! Do you know anything about it?" asked Charlie.

"What do you mean?" asked Uncle Eli.

"For the past two nights, I've seen a red glow and heard moaning in the shack," explained Charlie. "I thought about going to check it out, but it stopped before I could talk myself into going out in the storm. I remembered what you said about not going out after dark."

"Thank goodness you stayed inside!" said Uncle Eli.

"Why?" asked Charlie. "You do know something about it, don't you? What was out there in the shack?"

"Something you wouldn't want to meet up with," said Uncle Eli.

"What is it? Why didn't you tell me if something dangerous is here?" Charlie wanted to know.

"I was afraid you wouldn't come if I told you the story,"
said Uncle Eli.

"You'd better tell me now!" exclaimed Charlie.

"I didn't believe there was anything around here that
would hurt you, but I got worried and came out to check. You
remember I told you that Sophie Damron used to invite some
of her friends up here to the cabin to camp and fish or have a
bonfire?" asked Uncle Eli. "What happened was kept quiet, but
I heard what really happened."

"Yeah," said Charlie. "What's that got to do with the
shack?"

"Something terrible happened during one of those camping trips," said Uncle Eli. "Six of her friends arrived after school
on a Friday afternoon. It didn't take long to set up camp and
gather firewood. Sophie had marshmallows to roast on the fire
and hot dogs with all the trimmings. When they finished eating, they decided to take a night hike back into the woods. It
was the worst mistake of their lives."

"Why?" asked Charlie. "What happened?"

Uncle Eli sat silent for a minute, reluctant to discuss that
night. Finally, he spoke.

"Everything was fine at first," he said. "Sophie had
brought strips of old, white pillow cases to tie to trees so they
could find their way back. They had put new batteries in their
flashlights so they could see the trail. They were having such a
good time that they walked back into the woods farther than
they had ever been before. They only stopped when a roll of
thunder warned them that a storm was coming their way. They

took a few more steps forward, thinking the storm was slow moving and they had time to get back to camp.

"Suddenly, they stepped into a small clearing. A patch of sky remained uncovered by the storm clouds, allowing them to see by moonlight something dark in the center."

"What was it?" asked Charlie. "Was it a mound or a hole or what?"

"A hole," Uncle Eli said. "Sophie walked toward it and turned her flashlight on it."

Uncle Eli paused before he spoke again.

"Then they witnessed something so scary it was unbelievable. A glowing red figure rose out of the hole. It was the shape of an average man, but it had red fangs sticking out. It moaned like it was in pain. The hikers screamed and ran back down the trail. The rain had started, and it was hard to see the strips they had tied to the trees.

"Sophie was closer to the thing than they were; she tried to run, too. Her friends looked back, but she had fallen, and the red thing just wrapped her up like a blanket. There was nothing they could do, so they ran back to the cabin and told her parents.

"Mr. Damron started into the woods when a loud moan sounded, and they all saw a red glow in the fishing shack. He turned and ran to the shack as the red glow vanished. He opened the door and found Sophie inside, sobbing over where the wood was stacked. She looked at her father without any hint of recognition in her eyes and began to scream hysterically. She's never been the same since that night. It's like that thing sucked her mind right out of her body!"

"Where is she now?" asked Charlie.

"The Damrons keep her at home. They hire special nurses to take care of her. They don't want curious people coming by just to gawk at her," said Uncle Eli. "They tell people that she is away at school."

"Is that why they sold the cabin?" asked Charlie

"Yeah," said Uncle Eli. "They had a hard time selling it when the story I just told you got around. I bought it because I didn't believe it at first. I thought they saw ball lightning and got scared. But after I bought it, I saw something that changed my mind. I was out here fishing one day. I let time slip away from me and stayed until it was dark. I decided to leave my pole in the fishing shack, and just as I opened the door, I saw a creature like I had never seen before. The huge, ugly red-fanged thing just appeared from nowhere!"

"Where do you think it came from?" asked Charlie.

"I told you it just appeared," said Uncle Eli.

"Do you think it was a space creature or what?" asked Charlie.

"One of Sophie's friends suggested that after their experience, but I didn't see any sign of a space ship or UFO landing," said Uncle Eli.

"Then you think maybe it's a monster that lives in the earth?" asked Charlie.

"Yes, probably," said Uncle Eli. "And it only comes out at night."

"I just had a horrible thought," said Charlie. "If there is one of these monsters living in a hole in the woods, there must be others! Where do you think they are?"

"They could be anywhere!" Uncle Eli answered. "Anywhere at all!"

"From what I saw, we know that one monster is still here," said Charlie.

Uncle Eli nodded.

"I had hoped it was one of a kind and had gone by now."

"That rotting corpse smell might be from one of its victims!" exclaimed Charlie.

They both stood silent for a moment, thinking of a red-fanged creature biting into a victim.

"Tell you what," said Uncle Eli. "I don't have anything to do for the rest of the day. Why don't I give you a hand and clean this place up? Then you can follow me back to the city. I've got plenty of work back at home that needs doing, too. You can stay at our house and help with that, too, if you want."

Charlie and her Uncle Eli spent the rest of the day clearing the area around the cabin and loading Charlie's things in her car. They glanced at the fishing shack from time to time, but neither had any need or desire to go inside.

"You know," said Uncle Eli, "I've had a generous offer from a real estate company to buy this property on Damron's Creek. I'm thinking I may sell it. I don't come out here very much. What do you think?"

"Sell!" responded Charlie, without the slightest hesitation.

They both laughed.

"Okay, let's go home," said Uncle Eli.

Charlie totally agreed.

The sun was setting behind dark storm clouds as Uncle Eli drove ahead of Charlie's car. Both were concentrating on their driving or they would have seen a red glow behind them coming from the old fishing shack for a few seconds. They turned onto the main road just as Red Fang sank back into the earth to sleep.

Eternal Spring

"**R**iley, run to the spring and bring me a bucket of fresh spring water to drink. It's a special day with Josh coming home," said Grandma.

"I just brought you one a few minutes ago," complained Riley.

"Well, it won't kill you to go get me another, will it?" Grandma asked.

"I suppose not," Riley told her.

Riley loved her grandmother very much, so she picked up the bucket and started down the hill. Grandma was busy breaking green beans as part of the welcome dinner she was making for Josh, who was coming home today. The fresh spring water tasted so good, and Grandma loved using it for special occasions! She couldn't remember a time when that spring had gone dry. It flowed, clear and thirst-quenching, all the time.

The spring on Grandma's farm was the coldest one Riley had ever seen. The water flowed from a hole in the hillside and pooled into a basin below. It was clear and fresh with no hint of sulfur that ruined so many springs in the area. Grandpa had built a spring box where he would sometimes hold milk and butter to keep them extra fresh.

Beyond the spring were woods with a clearing in the center where the old family cemetery was located. The spring always had a happy, bubbling sound of running water, but the woods were still and dark.

Riley spent her summers with Grandma and Grandpa and was often sent to the cemetery to pull weeds around the graves. She didn't mind the work, but she always had the strangest feeling that death was a being that was always watching her there.

Riley filled the bucket and carried it up the hill to her grandmother. The old lady took the dipper from the other bucket she kept on a bench on the porch. As Riley watched her take a long, satisfying drink, she was pleased with herself for making the trip to the spring.

"What time is Uncle Josh coming home today?" asked Riley.

"The bus gets in at three o'clock," said Grandma. "He'll be on it. Then it will take a few minutes for him to walk home."

"I'll go to the spring and get some fresh water for him just before he gets here," Riley offered.

"That would be very nice," said Grandma. "He always loves that spring water. I'm sure he'll be thirsty after his walk."

The afternoon passed quickly. Grandma kept busy cooking all of Josh's favorite foods. She was fixing green beans, mashed potatoes, corn on the cob, fried chicken, cornbread, and a blackberry cobbler. She hummed happily as she worked. Josh had been stationed in the Middle East and was finally coming home.

Riley volunteered to bring up another bucket of fresh water from the spring. As she approached the spring this time, she felt a chill in the air. The afternoon shadows were moving in around the spring, so she figured the chill was normal even on a hot summer day. That didn't explain away her feeling of uneasiness, though. Something was watching her from the woods by the cemetery, so she filled her bucket and ran up the hill, spilling part of the water on the way.

The minutes ticked by. Two o'clock came. Then ten after three. Riley and her grandparents became more and more excited.

"I'd better go to the spring and get some fresh water," said Riley. "His bus must be in by now."

"Yes, honey," Grandpa agreed. "He should be getting here just about the time you get back."

Riley hurried down to the spring with her bucket. The shadows seemed darker now. She was eager to fill the bucket and hurry back up the hill to see Josh, so she wasn't paying attention to her surroundings.

She felt a bite on her leg and whirled to see what had bitten her. In the process, her ankle twisted and took her to the ground. A copperhead was on the ground near her. She was usually aware of what was around her, but this snake was silent, deadly, and gave no warning.

She knew she had to get help, but her grandparents were up the hill well out of earshot. She tried to stand, but her twisted ankle couldn't support her weight. Her situation seemed hopeless, but she fought to call out anyway.

"Help!" she called. "Please help me!"

There was no answer. Even the woods were silent.

"Please help me!" she called again.

As the woods began to turn dark, she couldn't believe what she saw. Uncle Josh was there beside her at the spring.

"Don't be afraid," he told her. "I'm with you now. We'll go home together."

That was the last thing Riley heard.

Back at the house, Grandma and Grandpa saw a police car coming down the road to their farm.

"Maybe a police officer is giving Josh a ride home," said Grandma.

The car stopped, and they saw that the police officer was alone.

"Come in," said Grandpa. "What can we do for you?"

"I have some bad news to tell you," said the police officer. "There was a bus accident this afternoon about twenty miles out of town. Nine passengers were killed, including Josh."

"No!" screamed Grandma. "That can't be true! He just survived the war! He can't be killed in a bus crash!"

The police officer stayed to try to comfort them.

An hour of grieving passed before the old couple realized that Riley hadn't come back with the water.

"Oh, Lord," cried Grandma, "something must have happened!"

"I'll go to the spring and see what's wrong," said the police officer.

The police officer came back shortly. He had found Riley's lifeless body by the spring.

"The odd thing," he told people later, "was that she was smiling blissfully. I've never seen anything like it."

In the Fog

The job had seemed ideal on paper. Lots of students took summer jobs as nannies in order to travel and earn money for college the next semester. Elizabeth Alcot had taken this job with the Ramas, who were spending the summer at their beach house. She had always wanted to spend a summer at the beach, but her parents could never afford it. Now here she was, right out of high school, ready to enter college in the fall, and living her dream!

Her parents had been very supportive when she applied for the job. Her scholarships would cover most of her college expenses, but the money she earned from this summer work would help with extras.

Elizabeth had very little work experience, but this job sounded so easy! She would be taking care of one eight-year-old boy.

"Amar is a quiet child," Mrs. Rama told her in their interview. "He has been withdrawn since his twin brother, Hari, disappeared here last summer. We debated about bringing him here so soon, but he said he wanted to come. I hope we've done the right thing."

"If you don't mind telling me, what happened to his brother?" asked Elizabeth.

"He and Amar slipped out of the house one night to take a swim in the ocean," said Mrs. Rama. "They both knew they were breaking the rules, but they were both very strong swimmers, and I guess they thought they couldn't come to any harm.

"While they were out in the ocean, a dense fog moved in so quickly that they were caught before they could swim back to the beach. Amar doesn't know what really happened. He lost sight of Hari as the fog rolled in. He heard him scream, but when he called back, Hari didn't answer. Amar became disoriented himself. He started swimming, but he didn't know if he was headed back to the beach or out to sea."

"What a horrible experience!" exclaimed Elizabeth. "Did he find him?"

"That's an odd thing," she continued. "The fog lifted as quickly as it had come. The water was calm, and not a ripple or wave was on the surface. Amar began swimming toward the shore, calling for help, and we rushed out to see what was going on.

"My husband ran immediately to the water to see if he could find Hari, while I called the coast guard. I got Amar into warm clothes and blankets, then made him hot chocolate. I was afraid he would go into shock; he was shaking so much from the cold. He said the fog had felt like ice, even though it was a hot summer night. He also said he saw human-like figures reaching for him!

"Hari's body was never found. That makes it even harder!" Mrs. Rama's voice cracked, and she stopped talking.

"Please don't talk about it if it is too painful," said Elizabeth. "It must be so hard for you to come back here!"

"It's been really hard, but I'm all right now. We just have to take life day by day," said Mrs. Rama, wiping her eyes. "We will probably never know what happened. We just have to face it and move on. I told you all of this so you will understand if Amar is quieter than most eight-year-olds you know. I thought you should know all of this before you take the job."

"Thank you, Mrs. Rama," said Elizabeth. "I'll keep a close eye on him, and I'll make sure he stays safe. I definitely want this job!"

Mrs. Rama nodded.

"We'll pick you up in the morning at nine o'clock."

How lucky I am to get this job! Elizabeth thought. But as a chill ran through her body, another thought came to mind. *If I am really lucky, why do all my instincts tell me not to go?*

By bedtime that night, she was packed and ready to go. She had convinced herself that her fear had been the result of hearing that terrible story. It was enough to spook anyone.

The next morning when the Ramas picked her up, she was truly looking forward to going to the beach for the summer.

She met Amar for the first time on the ride down to the coast. He was polite but definitely quiet during the entire trip. They all pitched in to help unload the car and then looked about the house. It was furnished, and the cook kept the refrigerator and the pantry well stocked. She and the housekeeper lived close by, so the house was kept in order at all times. The Ramas only had to bring clothes and personal items.

"Do you need help carrying anything?" asked Mr. Rama.

"No, I'm fine," said Elizabeth.

Amar took his luggage and a box of games to his room and closed the door, leaving Elizabeth to carry her own luggage to her room. It was a lovely, big room overlooking the beach. She stood staring at the view. She could hardly believe that she would be spending the entire summer in such a beautiful place. A knock on the door interrupted her pleasant thoughts.

"Come in," said Elizabeth.

Mrs. Rama stepped inside.

"I've asked the cook to prepare a light dinner for us tonight, so you may eat in your room if you like. You'll have this evening to unpack and settle in. We won't need your services to begin until tomorrow morning when we have breakfast at 7:00 a.m. From then on, you'll take your meals with the family."

"Thank you," said Elizabeth.

"Good night," said Mrs. Rama, as she stepped out into the hall and closed the door behind her.

The sun was low in the sky, but Elizabeth decided to take a sandwich, chips, a soda, and an old magazine she found on the nightstand to the beach and relax a bit before she started unpacking. She changed into her swimsuit, grabbed her beach towel, and stopped by the kitchen to pick up her picnic supper.

She had planned to take a quick swim before she ate, but by the time she had reached the water's edge, the air had turned cold! It was much too cold to swim. She spread out her towel and began to eat her sandwich and chips. She sipped her drink and flipped through the old magazine. Something caught her eye. It was a story about a boat sinking near this beach many decades ago, but the bodies were never found.

Tragedy seems so out of place here, she mused.

The article in the magazine said that a ship carried an evil captain and crew. They would drop anchor offshore, and the captain would send crew members to capture people to sell as slaves! They were successful because they waited for the fog to roll in and conceal the boat that came to shore. One night, the coast guard was waiting in the fog and attacked the crew. The ship caught fire, and some of the crew jumped into the water. The ship sailed away and didn't try to rescue any of the crew left in the water. The fog was so heavy that the coast guard couldn't find any of the men. When it finally lifted, there was no sign of any of the crew. The story reported that their ghosts are still around, trying to grab people in the fog to sell as slaves!

What an awful story! she thought.

In the distance, low voices carried on a breeze seemed to agree with her.

As she finished her last sip from her drink, she noticed that the wind had picked up quite a bit. She looked out over the ocean and noticed that the fog was forming offshore. As it began to move toward land, Elizabeth suddenly became uneasy. The uneasy feeling quickly turned to panic, and she didn't know why. She just knew she had to get off the beach.

She grabbed the trash from her meal and stuffed it into the bag she had used to bring her food to the beach. She snatched up her beach towel and raced toward the house. She thought she heard a child's voice calling as she ran, but she didn't look back. It sounded like a young boy crying, "Help me!" A seagull flew over, and she thought she must have heard its cry.

Darkness had made its descent swiftly, and Elizabeth was relieved when she reached the beach house and entered safely.

She unpacked and vowed that she would not be caught on the beach at night again.

The next couple of weeks passed without any problems. Amar proved to be a good companion once he got to know her. He was even willing to accompany her to the library when the weather kept them off the beach.

On one visit to the library, Amar and Elizabeth browsed through the local folklore section.

"Look, Elizabeth," said Amar. "Here's a book about this beach."

He turned the pages carefully and stopped at one story that caught his eye.

"This story says that there are lost souls offshore, and they are looking for people to capture and sell. Where would ghosts sell slaves?" he asked Elizabeth.

"That's scary, even if it is just a ghost story!" Elizabeth answered in a reassuring tone.

Amar looked very thoughtful for a moment.

"Do you think one could have caught my brother?" he asked.

"Oh, no, Amar," said Elizabeth smiling. "These are just old tales. They are the kind of scary stories you tell when you're sitting around the fire on a stormy night."

"I don't know," he said very seriously. "Something was out there in the fog with Hari and me last summer."

"What do you think it was?" Elizabeth asked him.

"I couldn't see well in the fog, so I can't be sure. I think I saw hands grabbing at him when he screamed," he said. "I tried to get hold of him, but he just vanished! I tried to save him, but he disappeared in the fog."

"I believe you, Amar." Elizabeth touched his arm to comfort him. "You did all you could; it's not your fault that he vanished."

It was getting late, so they put the book back on the shelf and walked home in time for supper. Amar told his parents about the legend, but they didn't think it was very believable.

"You be certain that you are never on that beach at night again," ordered his father. "I don't think ghosts are out there, but you never know who might be lurking about!"

Elizabeth and Amar assured him that they had no desire to be out there at night.

As Elizabeth got ready for bed, she heard thunder directly over the house. Without warning, a violent storm took over the sky and raged around the house and on the beach. It must have approached while they were eating. It reminded Elizabeth about the legend Amar had found in the library book and the story she read in the old magazine.

When the storm blew itself out and the rain stopped, Elizabeth heard a foghorn way off in the distance. It was odd that she had not heard one before. She looked out the window and saw that fog had crept in.

As she watched, she was surprised to see Amar run from the back of the house and head toward the beach. The fog was rolling quickly in to meet him. She had to stop him!

"Amar's headed to the beach!" she yelled as she passed the living room where the Ramas were watching TV. She knew she might need help in handling the situation.

She ran out the front door and headed in the direction Amar had gone. He was already shrouded in the fog before she caught up.

Mr. and Mrs. Rama grabbed their jackets as they chased after Elizabeth. By the time they reached her, she had already stopped where the fog ended.

"Where did he go?" they asked her.

"He ran into the fog," she told them, "but I can't imagine why he would do that."

"Amar!" Mr. Rama called. "Where are you?"

No reply came.

"We'll go left, and you go right," Mrs. Rama directed Elizabeth. "Stay out of the fog, and keep calling!"

They hurried away in opposite directions.

"Amar! Amar!" they yelled, but he didn't answer. He had to be close enough to hear them, but he seemed to have disappeared without a trace.

Then, only for a second, the fog thinned out. Elizabeth could see a figure struggling with Amar.

"Stop!" yelled Elizabeth. "Let him go!"

She ran into the fog and grabbed Amar.

"It's too late," said the dark figure.

Mr. and Mrs. Rama heard Elizabeth's shouting and ran out to help her. As they approached, she gave one last yank, and Amar was free! Mr. Rama picked him up, and they hurried toward the house. As Elizabeth followed them, she heard the figure laugh.

"You don't think you really saved him, do you?" she laughed. "He'll come back. They always do. They can't resist the beaches. And we're not only on this beach, we are all along the shoreline of every beach, just waiting in our watery graves for the fog to move in so we can continue our work." Then Elizabeth thought she heard the woman's voice laugh again as she faded into the foggy mist.

Elizabeth tried to blot the dark figure's words from her mind as she stumbled up the sand bank toward the house. She hoped desperately that she could convince the Ramas to leave before the fog once again swallowed another victim.

Welcome to
Your New Home

The Feathered Thing

Piercing screams woke the Newtons from a deep sleep.

"That's Jo," gasped Mrs. Newton, throwing the covers back and racing down the hall to her daughter's room. Mr. Newton was right on her heels.

They threw open the door and hurried to their daughter's bedside. She was sitting up in bed with her face buried in her hands, shaking and sobbing. Her half sister, Sandy Piper, was sitting up, too, but she had turned her bedside lamp on and was watching quietly. If the Newtons had looked closely, they would have noticed the amused look twinkling in her eyes. But they didn't notice. Mrs. Newton sat on the side of Jo's bed and put her arms around her. Mr. Newton stood looking down at them.

"What's wrong, honey?" he asked Jo.

She looked up at him with tears of fright still creeping down her cheeks.

"Sandy Piper has a bird in that box by her bed! She knows I am scared to death of birds!"

"Is that true, Sandy Piper?" asked Mrs. Newton. "Do you have a bird in that box?"

"It's hurt," said Sandy Piper defensively. "I want to keep it until its wing heals. It's a school project for my science class. My teacher said it was okay. Jo doesn't even have to see it."

"Dad, she brought it to my bed and shoved the open box right in my face! She laughed when I started screaming! She jumped back in bed when she heard you and Mom coming!" cried Jo.

"That's a lie!" shouted Sandy Piper. "I did not!"

"Yes, you did! You're the one lying!" Jo shouted back.

"Girls, let's all go back to bed. We'll settle this in the morning," suggested Mrs. Newton. "Jo, I think you'd better sleep in our room tonight."

"But this is my room, Mom!" Jo protested.

"It's just for tonight," she said. "We'll straighten things out in the morning."

As Jo followed her parents from her room, she looked back at Sandy Piper. Sandy Piper smiled smugly and stuck out her tongue.

"Did you see that?" Jo asked her father.

"No," he answered. "Forget about Sandy Piper and go with your mother. I am going down to get you a glass of warm milk while Mom gets you settled in.

Mr. Newton went down to the kitchen to get the milk, and Mrs. Newton tucked Jo in snugly on the small couch in their bedroom.

"There, now," said Mrs. Newton. "Are you okay?"

Jo shook her head.

"Why did Sandy Piper have to come live with us?" she asked her mother. "I don't like her."

"Honey," replied Mrs. Newton, "Please give her a chance. She's your half sister, and when her mother died, she had no place to go but here. She's part of our family now. Aren't you happy to have a big sister?"

"No," said Jo. "She doesn't like anything I like!"

"You will find that you have more things in common as you get to know each other better. Think about how she feels. It is hard for her to fit in," said Mrs. Newton.

"She's weird, Mom," said Jo. "I don't like her, and the kids at school don't like her either. I don't think she cares much about fitting in. And I know she doesn't like me, either! She's always saying she comes from a family of witches and warlocks. She said her grandfather knows magic. She even said that one night she will have him send a big feathered thing to come and take me away where nobody will ever find me!"

"She was just teasing you," said Mrs. Newton.

"Why didn't she ever come visit us before?" asked Jo.

She was waiting for her mother to answer when her father walked into the room with the milk.

"I can explain that," her father said, handing her the glass of milk. "Her mother took her to her grandfather's house in Salem, Massachusetts when she and I divorced. I tried to see Sandy Piper, but her mother made it very difficult. I could only see her in Salem. Her mother was ill, and Sandy Piper wanted to stay close to her."

"Did she really come from a family of witches and warlocks?" Jo asked. "She tells the kids at school that she did. She wants the kids to think I'm as weird as she is!"

Her dad smiled.

"Her grandfather owns a magic shop and bookstore," he said. "I think she likes to make up tales connected with that. I only met him a couple of times, but he looked harmless enough to me."

Jo sipped her warm milk and asked more questions.

"Why does she have a funny name like Sandy Piper? She said she was named for a bird."

Her dad laughed and sat silent for a moment as if remembering. He had a far-away look in his eyes when he answered.

"When Sandy Piper was born, we originally named her Sandy. For about six months, she cried and cried, and we couldn't figure out what was wrong. The summer after she was born, we took a family trip to the beach. Sandy loved the sandpipers! When we placed her by the birds, she'd stop crying immediately. Her mother started calling her Sandy Piper as a nickname, and it stuck."

"That's silly," said Jo.

She finished her milk and opened her mouth to continue questioning her father, but he spoke before she could get the words out.

"Enough talking for tonight," he said. "Now go to sleep!"

"I'll bet she gets to stay awake," pouted Jo. "She's taken over my room, and I don't want to be in there with her anymore!"

"Don't get your feathers ruffled, Jo!" laughed her dad. "We're fixing up a room for her upstairs."

"I hate feather jokes, and I hate living with her, Dad!" Jo said, raising her voice.

"That's enough, Jo," said Mrs. Newton. "Now settle down and go to sleep!"

Morning tiptoed in quietly. The family gathered in the kitchen for breakfast. No one was in the mood to talk. All was silent until the THUMP against the sliding patio door. A bird had flown into the glass door and now lay dead on the patio. Jo began to cry hysterically. Mr. Newton hurried to close the drapes and remove the dead bird. Mrs. Newton was trying to calm Jo when Sandy Piper offered a suggestion.

"Maybe you should take her to the aviary at the zoo. Or you could suggest that the science teacher take the class on a field trip. My mom always said it is better to face our fears."

"That's something worth considering," said Mrs. Newton.

Jo had calmed down to occasional hiccups now.

"What's an aviary?" she asked.

"It's a huge room where birds are confined," explained Mrs. Newton. "They are not in cages, though. They are free to fly around. The one at the zoo even has a real tree growing in it."

"It sounds horrible!" Jo said to her mom. "Please don't ever make me go there!"

The dreadful incident had ended breakfast, so everybody went their separate ways to carry out their plans for the day. To Jo, the day dragged on forever. The mood at home was definitely subdued. The family said little during dinner or before bedtime. Jo picked at her food. Every bite tried to come back up when she thought of that dead bird. She was developing a slight headache.

"I'm not feeling very well," she told her parents. "Is it okay if I take a shower and go to bed?"

Both nodded, and Mrs. Newton looked in a little later and saw that Jo was sleeping soundly.

Sandy Piper read for a while and went to bed at the same time the Newtons turned in. A grim silence crept over the house. Everything was on hold, waiting and listening for the first sign that life as they knew it would soon be over.

When it came, nobody heard it but Jo. A pecking at the window roused her from sleep.

Sandy Piper is trying to scare me, she thought. *I'll pretend to be asleep.*

She carefully moved the cover back from her eyes and peeked across at Sandy Piper's bed. She wasn't moving, but she was probably faking sleep, too.

Swoosh!

Jo responded by glancing at the window. The light from the moon provided a pale backdrop as some huge, shadowy bird glided past the window.

Then things happened too quickly to be interrupted.

The shadowy thing floated through the closed window as if the window weren't there and settled on Sandy Piper. Jo watched as if she were frozen in a nightmare. She expected Sandy Piper to scream, but she didn't! Sandy Piper blended with the awful creature, and it rose and glided toward her. Her mind ordered her arms up in self-defense, but they would not obey. The feathered thing landed on her before she could move or scream.

This is not happening, she thought. *This can't be! It's a bad dream! I'll wake up any second now!*

The thing spread its wings and covered her. A painful peck to the forehead made her realize that she wasn't dreaming! The thing looked into her eyes, and she looked back—right into the eyes of her half sister. Another peck to the forehead and Jo felt weightless. Everything went dark.

Jo didn't know how much time had passed when she finally woke up. She only knew she felt very different and that she was not in her own bed. She had no way of knowing that her parents had found her bed empty and were searching frantically for her.

Gradually she heard chirping and swishing. The air was full of wings! Where was she? What was going on? Her eyes were not working right, but they cleared enough to show her she was surrounded by birds, flying freely all around her. It was too horrible to bear! She tried calling for help, but her voice only cheeped and trilled!

Mom! Dad! Anybody! Please help me! she thought. She wanted to go home! She knew it was hopeless, though. Sandy Piper had told her this would happen. She had made sure her prediction would come true. That wicked girl had won!

Maybe she would have a chance if her science class came for the field trip! But Sandy Piper would never mention it now, and her mom would never think of it again.

Despair enveloped her. She would never see her home and her parents again. She would never go back to school or see her friends. No one would ever find her here in the midst of all these birds! Who would notice the new little feathered thing clinging frantically to a limb on the real tree in the zoo's aviary?

The Nest

The Morabito family rounded the curve and saw the sign for the Dark Mountain Bird Sanctuary on the left just ahead.

"Wow!" said Carlos. "Look at those trees! I've never seen trees so tall or so thick!"

"Me neither," said Mrs. Morabito. "What a great place for birds!"

"They cover the whole mountain," said Carlos. "Is that why they call this place Dark Mountain?"

A shiver ran up his spine when he asked that, and he had a brief, strong foreboding that the mountain was something to fear.

"That may be one reason," answered his dad, "but I think the real reason is that much of the mountain is unexplored. It seems mysterious and dark."

"Why did you want this job, Dad?" Carlos asked. "Aren't you afraid to be in charge of a whole mountain?"

"I think the mountain pretty much takes care of itself," Mr. Morabito told his son. "I really wanted to get us away from the city. Crime is increasing and life goes by too quickly. There's danger everywhere. I wanted to move us closer to nature where we'll be safe and life is peaceful."

"Like building a new nest," laughed Mrs. Moribito. "We'll be able to make our new home exactly the way we want." After years of high-pressure work as an accountant, she was looking forward to getting closer to nature and living a simpler life.

"When will we get to explore the mountain?" asked Carlos.

"Soon, but only certain parts of it. The owners of the Dark Mountain Bird Sanctuary have allowed scientists to place cameras and other equipment in designated areas to gather data and survey the area. I'll need to check on the equipment and cameras and keep everything running. We'll find plenty of time to do a little exploring of our own, though!"

"Wouldn't it be great if we discovered a new kind of bird?" Carlos said. "Do you think there might be birds in there that nobody knows about it?"

"I doubt it," said Mr. Moribito, "but it's possible. This mountain has been here since ancient times. There are no trails leading to some of the back areas. Remember, don't ever go exploring alone."

They turned into the sanctuary and got their first good look at their new home. It was a one-story house that ran along the side of the mountain and blended in easily with the trees. It seemed to be an extension of the foot of the mountain, which towered over the house. Carlos couldn't decide if the mountain looked more like a menace or a protector. He didn't know at that moment that he would soon learn the answer.

The next few days were uneventful. The movers unloaded the van and drove away. The Moribito family looked around their new home and unpacked. The master bedroom and bath were in the front of the house. That was fine with Carlos because his room and bath were in back facing the woods. He sat by his window with the light out and watched every shadow and movement, and listened for every sound among the trees. At dusky dark, he heard sounds and birdcalls that he couldn't identify. The sounds faded out as night came on. The absence of the city noises he was used to made it hard for Carlos to sleep.

"I'll be going up the mountain tomorrow morning to check the cameras and equipment," said Mr. Moribito.

"Will you take me with you?" asked Carlos.

"Not this time, Carlos," he said. "I need to see how rough the area is first. I want you to stay here and keep close to the house."

"Aw, gee, Dad," Carlos said, but he knew it was useless to argue.

His dad left early, and Carlos sat by his window and watched the woods for a while. His mom did the laundry and went outside to hang the clothes on the clothesline.

Carlos was getting tired and was thinking about going to the kitchen for a snack when a huge shadow passed over the yard. He tried to look out the window and see what it was, but whatever caused the shadow was just out of his line of vision.

He ran outside and looked up, but it had already disappeared in the woods on the mountain.

"Mom," he called. "Did you see that?"

"I saw a shadow, but when I looked up, it was gone," she said.

"Was it a bird?" he asked.

"I think it was too large for a bird," she said. "Maybe it was a glider plane or something?"

Carlos didn't think so, but he let the subject drop.

As soon as his dad came home, Carlos and his mother told him about the huge shadow.

"I don't know what it could be," he said. "Maybe it was a drone."

They ate supper in silence, but the shadow was very much on their minds when they went to bed. They woke up still thinking about it.

Mr. Moribito went back up the mountain that morning, but Carlos didn't ask to go along. He wanted to see if the shadow passed over again. He sat outside on the grass and waited. This time, he was rewarded for waiting patiently.

In late morning, the sky over the yard turned dark. Carlos looked up and saw the most terrifying thing he had ever seen, even more terrifying than his worst nightmares. The biggest bird he had ever seen flew right overhead and disappeared into the woods. It was carrying something in its mouth.

It must be a mother bird taking food to her babies, Carlos thought. *Her nest must be on Dark Mountain.*

Carlos stood rooted to the spot for a minute, and then fear propelled him through the back door.

"Mom, I saw it!" he shouted. "It's a bird! I never saw anything so big! It was carrying something in its mouth. It must have babies in a nest on the mountain."

"Stay inside, Carlos. We'll tell your dad when he gets home. Maybe he will have an explanation," she told him.

When Mr. Moribito came home, he was very skeptical of their story.

"Carlos, there are no birds as big as the one you've described; it's not possible," he said. "I think you let your imagination get the best of you."

"Dad," protested Carlos, "I wasn't imagining it. It looked almost as big as the birds pictured from dinosaur times."

"Impossible," said his dad.

Carlos didn't say anything else about it. He vowed to himself to try to get a picture of it, though. That would convince his father.

When his dad left to go up the mountain the next morning, Carlos took out his camera and waited outside for the bird. He moved out from the house into the open yard so he could have a better view. The only trouble was that the bird had a better view, too.

Suddenly, from out of nowhere, the shadow covered the yard. Carlos turned snapped a picture and sprinted as quickly as he could to the house. He made it inside just as a huge wing barely missed his head! When Carlos made it to the window and looked out, the bird was gone! Now he was certain that it must have a nest nearby.

He could hardly wait to show his parents the image he had captured. His mom turned pale when she saw it. His dad looked grim and was silent before he responded.

"Carlos, I don't want you going out of this house until we find out more about this thing!" he told him.

"I promise," said Carlos.

It wasn't hard to make that promise. He was too frightened to go out again.

"You be careful, too!" Mrs. Moribito told her husband. "What are you going to do about this bird?"

"First, I'll take this picture into town and check with the Dark Mountain owners. Maybe some of the cameras set inside the unexplored woods picked something up. I'll leave early in the morning, and I want both of you to stay inside this house every minute while I am gone! Agreed?"

They both promised him. They had no reason to go outside anyway.

Mr. Moribito left right after a hearty breakfast. Carlos and his mom faced a long day ahead. Carlos sat by his window to see the bird if it showed up again. His mom tried out a new dessert recipe and started on a stack of novels. About ten o'-clock, they both heard a horn sound out front. They looked out and saw the mailman in his truck by their box.

Mrs. Moribito opened the door and looked around quickly. "Can I help you?" she called.

"I have a package for you," he said, "but it is too big for your box. Can you come get it?"

Carlos dashed out the door before she had a chance to answer. He glanced up once, but the sky was clear. He took the package from the mailman and turned back toward the house as the mail truck pulled away.

Then the yard turned dark.

"Run, Carlos!" screamed his mother. "Hurry! It's the bird!"

Carlos ran! Suddenly it was swooping over him. He dropped the package and flung his arms about, trying to fight if off! His attempts, however, were futile.

Then it seemed to Carlos that the sky fell! Talons sank into his shoulders, and he was lifted from the earth in one swoop. He screamed as the pain seared through his body, and he prayed that the thing would not take him to its nest. Then everything went black.

His mother ran to the phone and frantically called for help.

Carlos woke surrounded by large, smooth stones. He didn't know what had happened at first, but slowly it all came back.

The bird was gone now. He needed to climb over these stones and get away before it came back. He had never seen anything like these stones before. They were not only bigger than a man, they were also smooth and speckled. He couldn't find a way to get a hold on any one of them to pull himself up. Three stones over, it looked like one of the stones was cracked and broken. He would like to check it out, but he had no time for investigating. That bird could return any minute, and he had to find a way to escape.

As he looked around to see the best way out, he heard a strange noise. He stood quietly and listened.

Peck! Peck! Peck!

The pecking was coming from inside the stones. It took a moment for the horror to sink in!

Suddenly, he realized that what he thought were stones were not stones at all. They were huge eggs! Now the young birds were pecking their way out of the eggshells, and Carlos soon saw that they were very, very hungry!

.

Silly Question

By the time the authorities found his Uncle Jomo and he agreed to take his nephew in, Anthony had come to terms with his parents' deaths.

First, there had been the funeral and the two weeks he had stayed with his neighbors after the car accident. It had helped to spend time with his best friend, Ezra, during those awful days.

Then he had been placed in a temporary foster home until Uncle Jomo had been located and arrangements were made for Anthony to move to his farm. The day his foster family told him about his new home, Anthony knew for sure that his parents were never coming back. Somehow his hope had lived on until then.

He had called Ezra to say goodbye and to give him his new address at Uncle Jomo's house. Anthony sounded very downhearted on the phone. Ezra was downhearted, too, but he tried to be brave about Anthony going.

"It's only seventy miles away," Ezra said, trying to cheer Anthony up. "And it's summer vacation now. I am sure Mom and Dad will drive me down to see you. And maybe your uncle will let you come to visit me."

That made Anthony feel a little better.

"I can still call you on my phone from Uncle Jomo's, I guess," said Anthony. "Also, he told me my friends can visit any time."

"He sounds pretty nice to say that," said Ezra.

"Yeah, I guess so," said Anthony. "I guess I'll find out how nice he is soon enough. I'll let you know."

The social worker in charge of Anthony's case drove him to his great uncle's farm. It was a much larger place than Anthony had imagined. His mom had mentioned her rich uncle a few times, but he had thought she was kidding about the extent of his wealth.

The large, two-story house looked like a mansion to Anthony as they turned down the driveway. He wished with all his heart to be back in the small house he had shared with his mom and dad. There, his room was right down the hall from theirs, and he could dash down the hall to their room if he got scared of anything. Now, he would never see the house or his parents again.

The driveway circled in front of the huge door, so the social worker stopped and helped Anthony get his few belongings out of the car. He held back briefly, knowing that when the social worker left, he would lose contact with the people who had made up his life before.

The social worker rang the bell, and Anthony moved closer to him as they waited.

A kindly lady in a maid's uniform opened the door.

"This must be Anthony," she said, smiling.

The social worker made the necessary introductions, and the maid led them into a beautiful sitting room to wait.

"Mr. Jomo will be down shortly," she said. "Could I get you something to eat or drink?"

"No, thank you," the social worker replied. "I have to be getting back soon. Would you like something, Anthony?"

Anthony was too nervous to eat or drink, so he just shook his head. It was probably good that he refused, because just then the door opened and in walked Uncle Jomo.

This man, who towered in the room at a good six feet four inches, would have frightened Anthony if he hadn't had such a kind smile.

Uncle Jomo nodded a greeting to the social worker and said, "Welcome, Anthony. This is Mrs. Carson, who runs this house for me. You will meet the rest of the staff later. Thank you, Mrs. Carson. You may go now."

"Yes, sir," she said. "Do you still want dinner moved up an hour from the usual time tonight?"

"Yes," said Uncle Jomo. "I'm sure Anthony is tired and hungry after his trip. We will make the change in his honor for tonight only."

"We've already covered the arrangements and the transition plan, so I'll be going," said the social worker. "Goodbye, Anthony. I know you are going to like your new home."

"Goodbye," Anthony said, wondering how he could make a judgment like that when he had only been in one room of the house for about ten minutes.

"Come along, Anthony," said Mrs. Carson. "I'll show you up to your room so you can get ready for dinner." She picked up two of the four suitcases Anthony had brought along and led the way. Anthony picked up the other two and followed her.

Anthony followed her upstairs, but he saw his uncle show the social worker to the door and exchange a few words with him before he left. An empty feeling engulfed Anthony as he watched the social worker go. He was truly alone now in his new world. There was no turning back—no other place for a lonely twelve-year-old boy to go.

At the top of the stairs, Mrs. Carson opened the door on the right and ushered Anthony into his new room. It was very large but cheerful. There was a full bath off of the left of his room. His bedroom had windows on two sides, so Anthony could see the front and side yard that led to the woods. He noticed a guest-house near the woods, and it appeared to be occupied.

"Who lives there?" asked Anthony, pointing to the house.

"The caretaker," answered Mrs. Carson, but she said no more.

"Where does everyone else sleep?" Anthony asked her.

"We all go home at night," she answered. "There will be no one here at night except you and your uncle. And the care-taker, of course, but he stays in his guest cottage at night."

"Where does Uncle Jomo sleep?" asked Anthony.

"His quarters are in the back on the second floor on the left," she said. "He likes a view of the woods and fields."

For some unknown reason, Anthony was relieved that he would not be sleeping on the second floor alone.

"Okay, let's unpack and settle in," she told Anthony. "The bell will ring for dinner at four o'clock. That's a couple of hours away. Please remember to come down on time. Mr. Jomo likes promptness."

"Does he have a last name?" Anthony asked. *That was a silly question,* he thought as soon as it was out of his mouth, but Mrs. Carson answered anyway.

"Oh, yes," she answered. "It's Okiro, like your mother's family, but he prefers to be called Mr. Jomo."

"Oh, yeah. Thanks! See you at four o'clock," said Anthony as Mrs. Carson closed the door and went downstairs.

Anthony explored the room before he began unpacking. His bed was on the side near the window. He liked that. He could lie awake at night and look at the stars.

Across the room near the bath was a huge walk-in closet. It had places for shoes, drawers in waist-high dressers for socks and underwear, and plenty of hangers for hanging up pants, coats, and shirts. There were several other places for storage.

He unpacked and put his things away. The room seemed a little more like his own after that. He had just enough time to shower and change clothes before running down to dinner. Uncle Jomo was already seated and waiting.

"Am I late?" asked Anthony. "I hurried down when I heard the bell."

"You are right on time," said Uncle Jomo. "I was already downstairs, so I had a head start on you. I hope you're hungry. Mr. Cook made some special food for you tonight."

"Is Mr. Cook the cook?" asked Anthony.

"Yes," his uncle said and smiled. "That's his name, and that is what he does. I guess that is funny to you."

Anthony smiled and nodded.

Mr. Cook entered with a platter of fried chicken. He left and returned time and again with a basket of hot bread, bowls of mashed potatoes, green beans, and buttered corn. A woman, whom he introduced as his wife, Mrs. Cook, brought in a pitcher of milk and set it on the table.

"Mrs. Cook has several jobs here," explained Uncle Jomo. "She is the general handy worker, gardener, and chauffeur."

"Here is apple pie and cheese for dessert," said Mr. Cook. "Will there be anything else?"

"No, thank you," said Uncle Jomo. "You may go now."

Anthony watched the Cooks and Mrs. Carson hurry to their cars and drive away. He turned to his uncle with a puzzled look.

"Do they always leave before you finish eating?" asked Anthony.

"Yes," said Uncle Jomo. "They need to be home before dark."

"Why?" Anthony asked.

"Eat now," said Uncle Jomo. "I'll tell you about it later."

"Do we have to do the dishes?" asked Anthony. *Another silly question,* he thought.

"No, Anthony. We leave them for the staff to do in the morning. Now dig in! The food is getting cold."

Mom never liked to leave the dishes overnight, he thought. *She said the food got stuck and was hard to get off. These people are odd.*

The food was delicious, though, and he gobbled it down in silence. He couldn't help but notice that the house became very quiet, too, and the silence made him very uneasy!

When they had both cleaned their plates, Uncle Jomo served the apple pie and cheese. Anthony thought it was almost as good as his mother's cooking.

"Thank you, Uncle Jomo," Anthony said, because being polite was what his mother had taught him to do. "Now will you tell me why everybody leaves before dark?"

"Yes," said Uncle Jomo, "but let's go into my study."

Anthony followed him down a hall to the back of the house. His uncle opened the door to what he called his study. Anthony could easily see why he would call it that. He could study anything he wanted in there.

Books lined two walls. Computers, screens, telescopes, microscopes, sound equipment, and other equipment Anthony didn't recognize was against another wall and on tables in the middle of the large room. The fourth wall was made entirely of glass.

Anthony walked over and put his face against the glass. The moonlight was bright, so Anthony could see that the glass wall looked out over the back yard, the caretaker's cottage, and the woods beyond.

Suddenly, from out of nowhere a face was pressed against the other side of the glass right in front of Anthony's face! It was black, with slanted green eyes and an open mouth full of sharp teeth. It was the biggest cat Anthony had ever seen!

"Hissss!"

It directed the hiss toward Anthony, as if it were speaking to him.

"Ahhh!" screamed Anthony, jumping back. "What is that?"

"That's Tom's Cat," said Uncle Jomo.

"What's its name?" asked Anthony.

"Tom's Cat," he answered. "That's all we've ever called it."

Tom's cat was now clawing and scratching on the window, frantically trying to get inside.

"MEOW!" it called out, sounding almost human.

"Is it going to get in here?" asked Anthony.

"The glass is unbreakable. You don't have to worry," said Uncle Jomo. "But that is why nobody ever goes out at night. And you must never go out either."

"Who owns that thing? Why don't you get rid of it?" asked Anthony.

"This farm and this village once belonged to Carmen Lopez," said Uncle Jomo. "She didn't farm the land. She used it as a base for her scientific experiments. I'm afraid some of them were on animals. Most people thought of her as a mad scientist.

"Her son Tom loved the land and all the animals, especially his black cat. He worked harder than anyone his age should have to work, but nothing he did ever pleased his mother.

"One day something happened that sent old Lopez over the edge. Nobody knows what happened between Tom and his mother. Tom never did say, but in a fit of anger, Carmen Lopez snatched up Tom's cat and took it into her lab. Nobody knows what she did, but the cat changed. It grew to triple its size, and it developed a very violent disposition.

"Poor Tom was crushed. He changed, becoming like a sad old man almost over night. Lopez sold the land and moved to the back of the woods. She left Tom on his own. When I bought this farm from Lopez, I asked Tom to live in the guest-house as caretaker. He's perfect for the job. I can depend on him to keep everything running as it should. He keeps to himself, though."

The cat was pacing back and forth outside while Uncle Jomo was talking. It turned and disappeared into the woods just as he finished.

"Does the cat stay with Tom now?" asked Anthony.

"Oh, no!" said Uncle Jomo. "Carmen Lopez kept Tom's cat. She takes great pleasure in turning it out at night to hunt. Two villagers were attacked before it became apparent that the cat was responsible. It clawed lips, ears, and eyes, and ripped faces."

"Can't someone take it away?" asked Anthony.

"That is the strange thing, Anthony," said Uncle Jomo. "Nobody can catch it! It's like a spirit cat. So just don't go out after dark, Anthony, and you will be perfectly safe. Now promise me!"

"I promise," said Anthony. "I wouldn't want to meet up with that thing."

"Good," said Uncle Jomo. "Now I guess we should both get to bed."

"Is it okay if I call my friend Ezra?" asked Anthony. "I promised I'd call and let him know how I am."

"All right," said Uncle Jomo, "but don't talk too long."

They walked upstairs together, and Anthony said goodnight as he went into his room. He heard his uncle walk down the hall and close his bedroom door. Anthony dialed Ezra and told him the incredible story about Tom's cat. He could still see the cat's face in his mind when he ended his call and went to bed.

After breakfast the next morning, Uncle Jomo showed Anthony around the farm. Tom Lopez was in the barn working and nodded hello to Anthony when the two walked by.

"He looks kind," Anthony said as they walked on.

"He is," Uncle Jomo told the boy. "He didn't deserve what happened to him."

As Anthony looked at the farm and the woods, which didn't seem so menacing in daylight, he wondered if maybe his uncle was making up tales to keep him from wandering about at night. Then he remembered that cat's face on the other side of the wall, and he knew the story was true.

Anthony began to settle into the routine at his new home. A few weeks passed. Uncle Jomo and the staff were kind to him. Tom Lopez began to talk to him about the animals. Anthony never dared mention Tom's cat, though.

Anthony texted Ezra almost every night and tried to call him once a week to update him about life on the farm. He had noticed, though, that for the last couple of nights he wasn't hearing from Ezra as much. Ezra would say he had homework to do, but he didn't seem as interested in Anthony's life now as he used to be.

Then the cat showed up again.

It was raining that night, so the cat appeared at the glass wall in the study without any warning. Anthony and Uncle Jomo were watching TV when the creature thumped against the glass. Anthony, feeling braver now that he knew the cat couldn't break the glass, ran over and stuck his tongue out at it. Instantly, there was eye contact. The cat was angry. It seemed to be warning Anthony that his action had been a dangerous one! For the first time in his life, Anthony stood there experiencing total terror.

"Come away from the window now, Anthony," his uncle commanded. "Don't taunt the thing."

Anthony was relieved and happy to obey.

The next day started like other days on the farm, but it certainly didn't end that way. Tom had allowed Anthony to help him with the animals that day, but he had gone to his cottage early because he wasn't feeling well. Anthony told his uncle and asked if Mr. Cook could make Tom some chicken soup. It turned out that Uncle Jomo wasn't feeling well either, so he had eaten some of the soup and retired to his room. The staff got in their cars and drove away.

"Take the soup to Tom now, Anthony," his uncle told him. "I want you to have plenty of time to get back to the house before dark."

"Do you need anything before I go?" asked Anthony.

"No, thank you. I am getting sleepy now. I want to rest," he said.

Anthony went to the kitchen and found that Mr. Cook had already filled a container and left it on the counter. Anthony opened the door, picked up the container with both hands, and pushed the door with his foot. He didn't realize that the door didn't completely close.

Tom was grateful for the soup. Anthony stayed to see if Tom needed anything else. When he finally looked up, it was dusky dark.

"You had better stay here for the night," Tom said.

Anthony could see that Tom was sleepy now and needed to be left alone. Anthony thought if he hurried, he would still have time before real darkness came.

He closed Tom's door and began to run toward his great uncle's house. It was totally dark as he ran inside and closed the door behind him. Then he realized how silent everything was, but it was silent for only a few seconds.

Something moved in the darkness of the kitchen. Anthony raced up the stairs and opened the door to his room. Something was right on his heels. He could feel its breath on his neck. It pounced on his back, knocking him to the floor. Then he saw Tom's cat over his face, ripping at him.

He flung it off, and the cat ran down the stairs and out into the night. Anthony needed help, but he couldn't make his uncle hear him.

He thought of Ezra. He'd call and somehow make him understand he needed help. He dialed and Ezra answered.

"Hello?" he said.

Anthony tried to speak, but the words wouldn't come.

"Anthony?" said Ezra. "Stop playing games. I know it's you."

Oh, please don't hang up, thought Anthony. *You are my only chance, Ezra.*

Again, Anthony tried to speak, but Ezra interrupted.

"Anthony, say something! You're not funny anymore! What's the matter? Cat got your tongue?" laughed Ezra.

Anthony didn't answer such a silly question. He couldn't, because that was exactly what had happened.

Snow Flakes

"**I** wonder if we can sue the real estate company for not telling us about this place's history before we bought it?" asked Marco Bosko. "Isn't there a law about disclosure or something?"

"Marco, don't be silly!" his wife, Ellie, answered. "That's just an old tale about this place. I think they have to tell you if you buy a house where a murder has been committed. But old man Bruno wasn't a killer. He just wasn't always in his right mind at the end of his life."

"Not always in his right mind!" combated Marco. "He was a total flake! He didn't like the house decorated for Christmas. He said the earth should be decorated outside only. Decorating houses was not natural. His housekeeper said he would go out barefoot in snow and roll around trying to make snow angels. Then he would come in tracking snow and melting ice all over the kitchen floor!"

"That's just a tale!" insisted Ellie. "He would have had frostbitten feet if he had done that."

"The housekeeper said Bruno didn't stay out long enough for that, but it was long enough to make a mess," said Marco. "Then, he would run through the house tearing down all the Christmas decorations. It nearly drove his family crazy. He chanted about the power of nature, and then electrocuted himself by touching a defective string of Christmas lights that was supposed to have been thrown away the year before."

"I don't think so," Ellie insisted.

"It's true," said Marco. "He had been outside in his bare feet again, and he was standing in a puddle of melted snow when he picked up the string of lights. Now his ghost comes back and haunts this house!"

"That's ridiculous!" Ellie said, laughing. "Why would he do a thing like that?"

"The housekeeper said he liked to convert people to his way of thinking. He wanted them to become as flaky as he was and do the silly things he did at Christmas. The housekeeper couldn't keep decorations up at Christmas as long as he worked in this house!" explained Marco.

"Marco, I don't want the children to hear such nonsense," Ellie told him. "This is our first Christmas in our new house, and I want the children to have a Christmas they will remember. I don't want them thinking that some old ghost is going to come around tearing down their decorations. This is the first time we have had a house big enough to decorate like this."

She stopped and admired the tall Christmas tree. "I think Robby and Klara are too young to deal with the idea of ghosts."

"Well, of course I'm not going to tell the children," Marco answered. "The children might hear about it somewhere else, though, especially with a big snow predicted. We need to be ready with answers if they have questions."

"Okay," Ellie agreed, "but only if they ask."

The subject was dropped as the children came in from school on this final day before holiday break. They were in the mood to celebrate already.

Dinner was a very festive occasion that night. Ellie had made special goodies, and the children were allowed to have more dessert than usual. They chatted merrily among themselves until they heard the noise.

THUMP!

The sound at the front door silenced the family at the table.

"There is someone out there," said Marco, looking at Ellie.

"I wonder why they didn't ring the door bell?" Robby wanted to know.

"I'll go check," said Ellie.

She opened the door, but nobody was there. She looked all around and up and down, and then she spotted the reason for the thump.

"It's the wreath," she said, picking it up and placing it back on the door. "I guess the wind blew it off."

Marco kept quiet and resisted the urge to tell her that no wind or snow was predicted until after midnight that night.

She came back to the table, and they finished dinner without further incident. Then they played games and put their two children to bed.

The snow came at midnight, quietly covering the town like a downy blanket. The flakes fell and formed drifts along the backyard fence. Ellie and Marco opened the curtains and watched for a while before they fell asleep. Peace reigned—for a little while. Marco woke once and thought something had moved in the living room. He listened and heard nothing else.

I must have been dreaming, he thought, and quickly fell back to sleep. Ellie stirred briefly but never completely woke up. Temperatures plunged, and they snuggled close under the covers. It was the sounds of children playing outside in the snow that woke them in the morning.

Marco knew before he looked that it was Robby and Klara. He shook Ellie awake.

"Wake up! Hurry!" he said. "The children are outside."

He ran to the back door as quickly as he could.

"Robby! Klara!" he shouted. "Come inside this minute!"

Ellie grabbed her robe and caught up with him as he ran out the door.

It was worse than they thought. The children were in their thin pajamas without any shoes. They were building a snowman.

"This is Mr. Bruno," mumbled Klara, with her teeth chattering. She could barely speak, and she was turning blue from the freezing temperatures. "He said we could come outside and play with him."

Ellie and Marco carried their children inside and called 911. They frantically tried to revive their children as they waited for the ambulance to come. Then Marco glanced at the floor.

"Ellie, do you see that?" he asked.

"Yes," she nodded.

There on the floor was a puddle of melted snow, and there were footprints of bare adult feet walking out of it. They didn't have to follow the footprints to know that their decorations in the living room had all been destroyed.

The ambulance came, and sirens wailed. Doctors worked on the two children with everything they had, but it was too late. They had been exposed to the freezing cold too long. They died early Christmas morning.

"Maybe we should have warned them about the ghost," said Marco. "Maybe they wouldn't have followed him out."

"Don't torture yourself," Ellie told him. "How could we know such a thing was possible?"

Decorations never went up again in the Boskos' house. Old Bruno won that battle! People who sent the couple Christmas cards would get them back unopened, marked, "Return to Sender."

The strangest thing happened whenever it snowed on Christmas Eve. People would be awakened from their sleep by the laughter of Robby and Klara Bosko, dancing in their night-clothes on the lawn around two child-sized snow angels.

"Totally flaky," the neighbors would say and go back to bed. The deadly, cold snowflakes would settle on the earth, waiting for other victims.

Mark My Words

All the furniture and boxes from the moving van were now inside the house on Bon Hollow Road on the outskirts of Central City. As the van lights vanished in the distance, the Murphy family—Tyler, Gabrielle, and their twins, Brandon and Alyssa—stood in their front yard, watching it go and wondering if they had done the right thing by moving here.

The usual reasons went through their minds. The house was in good condition, the location was perfect for work and school, and the price had been well within their budget. Yet the house had one drawback that bothered them. Their house sat between the graveyard and the little country church.

"You won't like living here," said a voice behind them. "Mark my words!"

They turned and looked to see who had spoken. It was a dark-haired boy, about twelve years old, but there was a look in his eyes that was much older than twelve. The most disconcerting thing was the fact that he was leaning on the graveyard fence.

"Who are you?" asked Alyssa.

"Jayden Von Brandt," he said. "I used to live in this house."

"Where do you live now?" asked Mrs. Murphy.

"I had to move in with some other people," said Jayden.

"Why?" asked Brandon. "Did something happen to your family?"

"They burned to death here," Jayden answered, as calmly as if he were talking about the weather. "It happened while they were in their beds sleeping."

"Here?" asked Mr. Murphy. "In this house?"

"Yes," replied Jayden. "It's been remodeled. Didn't the real estate agent tell you?"

"No," answered Mr. Murphy. "He left that little detail out!"

"Did he tell you that this used to be Bone Hollow Road instead of Bon Hollow Road?" Jayden continued.

"No! Why did they change the name?" asked Mrs. Murphy.

"Because it leads to the graveyard where all the bones are," said Jayden. "I guess people didn't want to live on a road named Bone Hollow."

Shocked at this information, the Murphy family all looked at each other. Mr. Murphy thought that it was against the law not to disclose information of that nature to prospective buyers. At that moment he wondered if he could get his family's money back. His instinct told him he and his family should leave without even unpacking!

"That's awful about your family," said Brandon. "Why weren't you killed, too?"

"I wasn't there," he said. "I used to slip out at night with my telescope to look at the stars. That's what I was doing that night. I was on the other side of the graveyard when I saw the flames. I ran home right away, but I couldn't save them."

"Oh, my! What a horrible experience for you!" said Mrs. Murphy. "Do you have any other family?"

"No," he said. "I'm in a group home now. I guess I'd better get going so they won't worry about me."

"Well, come back and visit if you want to," said Mrs. Murphy. "Bye, now."

"Bye!" he said. "You won't like living here!"

The Murphy kids and their parents waved, and they all went inside to start the huge task of settling in.

"What a strange boy!" Mr. Murphy remarked.

When they glanced out the window, Jayden was nowhere in sight.

That evening, Mr. Murphy and Alyssa drove into town and bought take-out pizza for supper while Mrs. Murphy and Brandon unpacked enough dishes for them to use for that meal. They were so tired from moving that they all slept well that night. It was the last time they would sleep well in that house!

The next day, the Murphy family unpacked, shopped for groceries, and finally went to bed looking forward to a peaceful night.

At 2:00 a.m., Brandon woke to a noise in the closet. He sat up in bed and could see that a light was coming from under his closet door.

I didn't leave a light on in there, he thought.

He quietly got out of bed and tiptoed to the closet door. He took a deep breath and jerked it opened. He expected Alyssa to jump out and try to scare him, but nobody was there. Somebody must have been in there, though, because his clothes were all off the hangers, piled on the floor. He didn't think Alyssa would do that. There had to be some other explanation.

He darted from his room and pounded on his parents' door. "Hurry!" he shouted. "Come look in my closet."

He ran back to his room with his parents and his sleepy sister following.

They were as bewildered as he was by the pile of clothes on the closet floor.

"Did you hang them up right?" asked Alyssa.

"Of course I did!" he replied. "Now I've got to hang them all up again."

"Leave them until morning," suggested Mr. Murphy. "Let's go back to bed and try to get some sleep."

They attempted to sleep, but tossed and dozed off and on until morning.

After breakfast, everyone was busy getting the house organized.

"Check your room for dirty clothes," Mrs. Murphy instructed Alyssa. "And ask your brother if he has anything that needs washing while you are at it."

Alyssa called out to her brother as she passed his room, but he said he had nothing dirty. She continued to her room and opened her door.

"Mom! Come quick," she called.

Her mom ran up the stairs, and her dad and brother hurried to see what was going on.

There, scattered all over her carpet, was black graveyard dirt!

There was no mistaking that the soil was from the graveyard because Mrs. Murphy had looked at it when they moved in, thinking how rich it would be for her potted flowers. She wouldn't dare use it, though. She had always heard it was bad luck to bring graveyard dirt into a house. She wanted to get the dirt out of the house as soon as she could.

"Alyssa, get the vacuum cleaner and vacuum that up," said Mrs. Murphy. "Then take out the bag and put it in the garbage. I don't want that dirt in the house."

The mystery of the pile of clothes and graveyard dirt made the Murphy family edgy.

Jayden Von Brandt appeared from time to time, but he was always in a hurry to get back to the group home. Brandon wondered if maybe he snuck out. They probably wouldn't want him to return to such a tragic site. These uninvited visits made the family edgy, too.

The annoying things continued. Every night, something strange and annoying happened while they were asleep. Dead flowers showed up on Mr. and Mrs. Murphy's bed one night without explanation. Several times the family awoke to the faint smell of smoke. They always checked the house, but they could find no reason for it.

One morning at breakfast Alyssa said, "I think we have a ghost!"

Mr. and Mrs. Murphy laughed.

"Who would be haunting this place?" asked Brandon. "The Von Brandt family?"

"Could be!" said Alyssa. "Or maybe Jayden is a ghost and haunts the place! Maybe he died in the fire, too!"

"Yeah," said Brandon. "He is one strange boy! But how would he get inside our house?"

"Maybe there are secret tunnels!" said Alyssa. "This is an old house!"

"I don't know about your ghost theory," said Mr. Murphy, "but I think there are details about this house that we don't know. I am going to check at the library today and see if I can find any stories about the Von Brandt family and this house."

Mr. Murphy was delighted to find several articles in the library's extensive files. He read about the fire and found a few details Jayden had left out. There was evidence that the fire had been deliberately set!

Even though the Von Brandt family had had no known enemies, the police had checked out everybody the family knew, looking for anyone who might have had a motive. Mr. Murphy was surprised that the police had considered Jayden a suspect!

Mr. Murphy decided that his next stop should be at the police station.

Mr. Murphy introduced himself to the police chief and told her about their experiences living in the old Von Brandt house. He told her about Jayden's visits and his statement that he lived in a group home close by.

"He seems like a nice enough boy, but there is something strange about him," said Mr. Murphy.

"You're right about one thing," said the police chief. "Jayden Von Brandt is one strange kid. His folks had to be on him all the time."

"I would appreciate it if you could shed some light on all of the strange things that have been going on," Mr. Murphy said.

"My files are public records," said the police chief. "Let me see what I can find out about the Von Brandt case."

Mr. Murphy was happy to see the police chief pull up a document on her computer. Maybe he could get some answers now.

"For starters, Jayden Von Brandt does not live in a group home near you like he said," the police chief related. "We questioned him about the fire, but we never had conclusive proof that he set it. He was already seeing a psychiatrist because of problems he had at home.

"He was defiant. He liked to go out alone at night to study the stars. He was fascinated by fire, and he was caught trying to set fire to the family garage. He was diagnosed with sociopathic tendencies! Apparently, he has no conscience whatsoever, so he doesn't feel remorse for his actions. Examinations showed that Jayden's many emotional and mental problems were too severe for foster care or group homes."

"Where is he now?" asked Mr. Murphy.

"He is a patient in a juvenile residential facility at the edge of town. Obviously, he has been getting out and visiting his old home," said the police chief. "I will alert them right away. I don't think you'll have any more trouble."

"How did he get inside secretly to pull those pranks on us?" asked Mr. Murphy.

"When they remodeled the house after the fire, they included several crawl spaces. He could have used one of them," said the police chief.

"Thanks, Chief," said Mr. Murphy. "I think my family will rest easier now."

Mrs. Murphy, Alyssa, and Brandon were shocked that Jayden had been considered as a suspect in his family's death. However, as the days passed, nothing else unusual happened, so life was normal again. The mental facility evidently watched Jayden closely now so he couldn't escape.

The Murphy family decided that their house was a good place to live and let their guard down. They had almost put Jayden out of their minds. But Jayden had not forgotten them. It was cold enough to turn on the heat now. The gas fireplace in the family room provided all the warmth the family needed as they stayed up late on a Friday night, watching a movie. The children fell asleep first. Then Mr. and Mrs. Murphy dozed off. They could not have been asleep long, but it was long enough for the unthinkable to happen.

Mr. Murphy woke first to a funny smell.

"Gas!" he shouted. "Gabrielle, wake up! I smell gas!"

Everyone was awake now. They all saw that the flame in the fireplace was not burning.

"Let's get the kids outside," said Mrs. Murphy. "I'll call the fire department."

"Don't bother," said a voice from the shadows in the corner of the room. Jayden stepped into the light holding several long matches. "I told you that you wouldn't like living here!"

"Wait!" yelled Mr. Murphy. "Give me those matches!"

"I think I'll just keep them," said Jayden.

Mr. Murphy lunged for the matches, but he wasn't quick enough. Jayden turned away, struck a match, and threw it into the fireplace. The explosion turned the house into a blazing inferno and drowned out Jayden Von Brandt's evil laughter.

Snow Coverings

Jennifer Land loved the city! She couldn't understand why her parents had warned her of so many dangers! Her mother said the city was dirty and wicked. Her father told her to beware and not trust anyone, because they were not always who they seemed to be on first impression.

"That's just how parents are," she told herself. "They are overprotective of their children."

Nothing they said could persuade her to live at home on the farm. She had been hired by Land's Bank—yes, her aunt was the manager, but she wasn't too proud to have her aunt help her get the job.

There were good benefits, though: holidays, vacations, and good working hours. The salary was more than adequate for her to rent a comfortable one-bedroom apartment overlooking a park, and close enough for her to walk to work.

She loved to sit by her living room window and watch people coming and going in the park. It was especially beautiful when the street and lamplights in the park came on during nights when there was fresh-fallen snow.

She hadn't made any new friends yet, but she was giving herself time. She had only been here in the city for six weeks. Meanwhile, she would enjoy watching the flow of people from her window.

She had walked through the park a couple of times in daytime. Nothing seemed sinister to her. There were some houses and a couple of apartment buildings like the one where she lived on one side. There were various businesses on two sides and the Epling and Hammer Laboratories directly behind the park.

She often saw children playing in the park at dusk and even later. She felt safe and peaceful in her neighborhood since the children were allowed to play outside.

She especially loved it when several inches of new snow fell, and the children gathered in the park to build snowmen. They paid close attention to details and made the snowmen look almost real.

The odd thing was that the snowmen would be gone the day after they were built. They had not been knocked over and they had certainly not melted in this sub-zero weather! It looked like maybe they had been hauled away, but it was hard to tell from her window.

The park looked like an enchanted wonderland, not like the pastures back home surrounded by barbed wire with cows mooing for their supper. She knew this Friday night was going to be special. She had made it home on time, and she was looking forward to a weekend at home, catching up on reading, laundry, and writing.

The weather service had predicted several inches of snow, and it arrived right on schedule. She fixed herself a grilled cheese sandwich and a bowl of hot tomato soup. She put it all on a tray and set it up by the window so she could enjoy watching the snow and the snow people, as she liked to call them.

She sat at the window, relaxing after she finished eating. She got up long enough to make herself a cup of spiced tea and was headed back to her chair when the phone rang.

She wasn't homesick, but she was always happy to hear her parents' voices. Her mother put the call on speakerphone so both of her parents could talk to her at once.

"I've been worried about you all day," said her father.

"Would you please tell your dad that you are okay?" her mother asked, laughing. "He is convinced that something is going to happen to you, and he's driving me crazy!"

Jennifer laughed and told them both as convincingly as she could that everything was fine. When their conversation ended, Jennifer went back to the window. She didn't realize how long she had talked until she saw about a dozen children building a snowman in the park.

I would love to see them do that up close, she thought. *I'll get my coat, hat, and boots and go say hello to them.*

Her tea was cold by now so she dressed warmly and walked outside into the snowy night. She walked across to the park and came up silently behind the children.

It wasn't as warm and cozy outside as the lights had made it look from her apartment. She shivered as the snowman builders turned to see who was there. In truth, the park was empty now except for the children and her!

None of the children spoke.

"I came to tell you that I admire your work!" she smiled. The children smiled back politely.

"Go ahead," she said. "I don't want to interrupt."

They turned away from her, and they continued to push the loose snow into a pile.

She was so cold, and the children were obviously giving her the cold shoulder, so she turned to go home. That's when the unexpected happened.

Before she knew what was going on, the children completely surrounded her. They took hold of her and ushered her back into the park and stopped at their snow pile.

"Hey, let me go!" Jennifer shouted, struggling. "What do you think you're doing?"

They didn't speak. They only held her tighter. Jennifer tried to get away, but she was outnumbered.

While most of the children held her, the others began picking up snow and covering her with it. It was icy cold, but they paid no attention to her protests. She didn't know why they were doing such a thing, but they were packing her in snow.

"The joke is over!" she cried. "I'll get sick from this. Let me go!"

Her teeth were chattering, and she couldn't feel her feet or her hands anymore.

The children never stopped until she was buried upright in the snow in the park. The low temperature tonight would keep her in place. Her last thought was that she must look just like a snowman.

The children were laughing now, and they started to speak.

"Epling and Hammer can pick her up in the van any time now," said a boy. "Let's let them know."

"They'll pay us more this time," said a girl. "Dr. Hammer says it's hard to find young women to experiment on in their lab."

If only she had been alive, she could have told her parents that she finally understood their warnings. It was too late now for her to heed her father's words, though.

Her father was right: people are not always what they seem!

The Warning

For Mariana Salinas, life couldn't get much better. She had just graduated from college with her teaching degree and had been hired for her first job in her hometown. It didn't matter that she would be teaching in a one-room school in the country. She had gone to school there herself and had loved every minute of it. For as long as she could remember, she had loved children and had always known she wanted to be a teacher. Now at last her dream was coming true!

It had been a stroke of good luck that she had been able to rent the old Clark place. Her parents had helped her with the deposit, but her new job would allow her to pay them back very quickly. The house was in excellent condition, but Mariana knew the family couldn't stay on after their only daughter was killed.

Mariana had always like the Clarks, especially their girl Katie. She was always smiling and had a greeting for everybody. What had happened to her had been unthinkable!

Mariana knew the story well, even though it happened while she had been away at college. The whole community had been up in arms. They had never been so furious about anything!

School had started early that fall, so there were lots of warm days left to enjoy. The children did not ride school buses, because they all lived close to the school, but many of them walked home together, laughing and talking. They were perfectly safe in groups or alone, for nobody would ever think of harming a child! But one particular autumn day was an exception.

School had ended at the usual time, and the students started walking home. Katie's siblings stayed after school because they had soccer practice. Katie walked with Gina and Claire Reese, who lived nearby. An older girl, Lydia Nicolo, usually walked with them, too, but she had gone home with a friend to spend the night.

Lydia's visit would cost Katie her life.

Around the corner, just out of sight in the pine thicket, Ryan Meadows was waiting. In school, Ryan Meadows and Lydia were engaged in an intense, ongoing battle of practical jokes. Lydia was an excellent trickster and often succeeded in spooking Ryan, sometimes scaring him a bit too much. Lydia had continued to think of the spooks as a game, but Ryan had slowly built up a powerful resentment. Ryan had decided that today would be the day he spooked Lydia, bad! After weeks of being scared at every corner of the school, Ryan felt belittled and powerless. He decided that today he would have revenge on Lydia to make up for his humiliation. He hid just out of sight in the pine thicket so he could see the girls coming. He was going to grab Lydia and pull her into the thicket!

Katie and the Reese girls came to a split in the road. To the right was the Reese farm, and to the left was Katie's house.

"Do you want us to walk home with you since your brother and sister are at school and Lydia is not here today?" asked Gina.

"We'd be glad to," offered Claire.

"No, thanks," said Katie. "It's just a little way. I'm not afraid."

"Okay, see you soon," said Claire, and Gina told her the same. Katie waved goodbye and started down the road to her home. They didn't know they were saying goodbye to her for the last time.

Ryan heard the girls' voices, but he couldn't make out what they were saying. He thought it was odd that he didn't hear Lydia and Katie talking. He didn't want to give away his position, however, so he remained hidden, assuming Lydia was with Katie.

He lunged out of the thicket and grabbed the girl. He shook her hard!

"Stop!" yelled Katie. "You're hurting me!"

Shocked, Ryan threw Katie to the ground.

"Where—where is Lydia?" he demanded to know. "Where–where is–is she?" he said.

"I don't know," sobbed Katie. "She went home with someone else!"

He felt a wave of embarrassment! Lydia had tricked him again, and he couldn't believe it! Anger surged through him!

"Liar!" he raged, as he kicked the side of her head.

Katie was very still now.

Ryan picked her up and realized her body was limp. "Ah! No! She's dead. No no no."

He dropped her body to the ground and ran to the edge of the pine thicket to see if anyone was watching. He was shaking from fear. *I'll be in trouble if they find me here,* he thought, and he ran frantically from the scene.

Back in the thicket, Katie slowly regained consciousness. "Momma! Momma!" she called.

Down the road at Katie's house, her mother heard Katie's call silently in her head. *Momma! Momma!* The words were so clear, she knew immediately that something was wrong. She ran to her husband and demanded they look for Katie. They called their neighbors, and they joined the search.

They found Katie right away, but the concussion and shock of the incident had been too strong. They had lost their Katie. The shock and sorrow that followed were unbearably painful. News spread through the community, and everybody knew of the tragedy by suppertime. When Lydia told the police how she and Ryan had been playing a series of increasingly dramatic scary pranks on one another, the police were able to trace the crime to Ryan, and along with the evidence they found at the scene, they were able to arrest him for her death.

It was a time for mourning, and the days passed in sorrow. Then a strange thing happened. Everyone in the Clark household—not just Katie's mother—began to hear Katie's voice saying, *Momma! Momma!* When they looked outside, they would see the figure of a man standing behind a tree in the yard, looking at the house. When the police arrested a hobo peeping in windows one night, some people thought little Katie's ghost might be warning them that someone dangerous was hanging around.

The family continued to hear Katie's voice calling until they couldn't stand it any longer. They had put their house up for sale, and Mariana had rented it. The Clarks moved far away to try and begin a new life.

Mariana thought of little Katie often in the days after she moved in and how much sorrow her family had suffered.

On the plus side, Mariana was thrilled with her new job. She loved teaching, and she had no real problem students. They trusted her and told her about everything that happened in the community.

"Did you know that the police arrested a peeping Tom?" asked Claire Reese.

"I heard about that," replied Mariana. "Is the person still in jail?"

"No," said Gina Reese. "We're scared, Miss Salinas. My parents heard that he broke into some houses over in Milltown before he showed up here. He hurt one woman, but he got away. My mom said the police are pretty sure it's the same man."

"He hasn't been seen around here again, has he?" asked Mariana.

"No, but that doesn't mean he isn't here," said Claire. "Nobody knew Ryan Meadows was dangerous until he killed Katie."

"Let's all agree not to be out alone," said Mariana. "And stay inside with your families at night until we are sure this man is arrested or leaves the area, agreed?"

They agreed immediately, but Mariana knew she couldn't stay with her family at night. They lived too far away. She would have to stay alone. She vowed to be very watchful, though.

She made sure her doors and windows were locked at night, but sometimes she didn't plan well enough to get home before dark. One night, just as she closed the door behind her, she thought she heard footsteps on the porch. She quickly locked the door and listened. All was quiet except for one sound—a girl's voice calling, *Momma! Momma!*

I must be crazy! I'm not really hearing that, she thought to herself.

Momma! Momma!

Mariana stood frozen in terror! Why would this voice be calling her? Didn't someone say the child's ghost tried to warn people of danger? Was she in danger? She had to call someone to help her, but to get to the phone, she had to cross in front of the window—and the drapes were open. She ran to one side of the window and closed the drapes. Then she peeked out from the side.

A shadow moved down by the driveway, but it was not clear who cast the shadow. Whatever had been there was obviously leaving. She went to the kitchen and made herself dinner.

She went to bed early and read for a while. She felt a little foolish now. She had let the students at school spook her. She turned out the lamp and was about to go to sleep when she heard a sound again.

Momma! Momma!

This couldn't be happening! Why would the child call out to her? Then it occurred to her that Katie must think her mother still lived in the house. She was trying to warn her of some impending danger!

Mariana reached for the phone on her nightstand, but there was no dial tone.

Momma! Momma!

The girl's voice was louder and closer this time.

Mariana got quietly out of bed. She heard a noise at the back door in the kitchen. In desperation, she grabbed her cell phone. This time she got a connection. She phoned the police and almost cried with relief when the officer answered.

"Someone is trying to break into my house," she whispered. "Please hurry!"

"Lock yourself in the bathroom if it is close by," the officer told her. "Don't come out until I tell you to. We've got a patrol car nearby. They're on the way."

Mariana did what the police officer told her to do, but she felt that time had stopped.

Then she heard footsteps come into her room. Maybe it was the police officer!

A man's voice said, "Come out of there!"

As she reached for the lock, a voice said, *Momma! Momma!*

Oh, no! she thought. *It's the intruder! If Katie hadn't warned me, I would have opened the door.*

She stood very still, hardly breathing, praying the police would come quickly. The intruder shook the doorknob. Sobs stuck in Mariana's throat. Then she heard the front door burst open.

"Hands over your head," shouted the officer. "Cuff him!" she instructed the other officer.

Mariana heard the officer take the intruder away.

"You can come out now, Miss Salinas," the officer said through the door.

Her hands were shaking so hard that she could barely unlock it.

"You're safe now," she said. "That man will be away for a long, long time."

Long after the police had gone and she had downed two cups of tea, Mariana was still shaking. Now it was with relief, not fear.

"Katie, are you here?" she asked softly. "If you can hear me, I thank you for saving my life! But please, go to the light now! Be happy! I'll always remember your warning."

A child's laughter filled the room—the happy laughter of a young girl.

"Goodbye, Katie," said Mariana.

She heard the laughter one more time before it faded away, but she never again heard the warning voice crying, *Momma! Momma!*

Things Aren't Always What They Seem

Costume Party

Greatstone High School was having a Halloween costume party for the first time ever. Usually they had an afternoon harvest festival, followed by a spooky play at night, but they were finally having an event that Dylan Hunter would feel comfortable attending.

The high school was located next to the temple and cemetery, with the library, the bookstore, and Rodney Robinson's Garage on the next block. Dylan's family lived near the school, so he did not have to ride the school bus. He was grateful for that. He didn't like all the noise and fighting that he'd heard about on buses. He liked to get home after school and lie around for a while reading or snacking.

Dylan never wanted to spend an afternoon at a fall festival looking at pumpkins, squash, apples, canned jellies, or relishes. He never bought any of those things. He didn't like to get wet bobbing for apples in the game area. But this costume party offered other possibilities.

The food refreshment committee had planned a little bit of everything. They had even managed to get local restaurants and bakeries to donate samples. Dylan Hunter loved to eat. This night was his!

Of course, he had to have the right costume. He always enjoyed mingling in all kinds of situations without people knowing his identity.

"Find something you will be comfortable in," advised his mother. "You will need something that won't restrict your movements."

"Yeah," said Dylan. "I was thinking of wearing a cape. I guess lots of kids will dress like a vampire, though."

"Probably," agreed his mom. "That would be a logical choice since vampires come out at night."

Dylan looked at his invitation again.

"Isn't it cool that the committee sent invitations to all the students?" asked Dylan. "The committee chairman, Lucia Graves, said vampires have to have an invitation to come inside a place, so they didn't want to leave anyone out in case we have some vampires in the class!"

"Lucia Graves must be the class clown," said Dylan's father.

"She is," said Dylan. "She says with a name like Graves, she's got to be funny. She asked us to bring our invitations to the costume party."

"Good idea," said his father. "We wouldn't want any vampires left out in the cold!"

"I've got to come up with a costume," said Dylan, "or I won't need the invitation."

"Well, you could go as a vampire," his mother said. "It would be an easy costume."

"No, I think you were right the first time," he answered. "Too many people will be dressed that way. They'll make everybody run and scream and cover their necks."

Dylan thought about it for a while and finally decided on something comfortable and ordinary. It was football season, so he would dress as a football player. He dressed and headed out into the night for fun and food!

"No necking, now," called his father.

"Aw, come on, Dad. Very funny!"

He heard his dad laughing as he walked away.

Dylan walked through the cemetery and past the temple. A couple of teachers, acting as chaperones, greeted him at the door. He smiled, returned the greeting, and walked inside.

The lights in the school gym were dim, but the music was loud. Dylan stood on the sidelines in the shadows and looked around for a couple of minutes. The gym was packed. All the Greatstone students must have come.

He hadn't eaten supper yet, so he was getting a bit hungry. He walked over to the food table and checked it out. He sampled a few items, but they were not as tasty as they looked.

The music was throbbing in his head.

Why do kids think that the only good music is loud music? he wondered. *Mom says they will all go deaf. She's probably right.*

A young girl sitting alone on the sidelines smiled shyly at him as he passed. She was wearing a '50s skirt and a turtleneck sweater. He didn't really know what her costume represented, but he didn't care much for the turtleneck.

He smiled back but kept walking. She looked the other way immediately, probably hoping someone else would come by and join her.

He saw a couple leave the gym and go out into the court-yard. They had the right idea. They were the ones his dad should have warned about necking.

He didn't want to go right out behind them and intrude. He'd let them find a place to be alone, and then he would go out for some fresh air and relief from the loud music.

He let several minutes pass. His mouth was dry and his ears were ringing, so he decided this was a good time to make his exit. He edged his way to the door and darted through without being observed. He quietly approached the couple kissing by the bushes near the main entrance. He was strong now with excitement. He made his move so quickly that they never knew he was coming.

He flung the girl to the ground with his strong left arm. She lay there dazed. He had to work fast, so he grabbed the boy with his right hand and pushed his head back with his left. His fangs emerged from his disguise, and he sank them in the boy's neck and drank long and deep! Not quite satisfied, he threw the lifeless boy down in a heap.

He pulled the girl to her feet. She was limp with fear, and he had to hold her up and bite her neck at the same time. He drank quickly because he was afraid someone else might come out and catch him. He took a last slurp and dropped her body beside the boyfriend. He wiped his mouth with his handker-chief and slipped back inside the gym.

He walked over by the door, away from the band, and leaned against the wall. It was a little quieter here. He stood watching the students dancing and mingling in the room until the music stopped.

"Your attention, please," Lucia Graves said into the mi-crophone the band had been using. "We will have a fifteen-minute intermission, and then we will select the winner of the prize for the best costume. Hold on to your invitations. We'll draw to see who wins."

Everybody headed for the food and drinks or the restrooms. Dylan knew this would be the best time to go home while everyone was milling around. He saw several couples go outside, and that was when the screaming started!

The commotion brought the teachers and other chaperones running to the scene outside. There were screams to call 911, screams for students to get back inside, and screams that had no meaning at all except to express the horror felt at the sight of two pale, bloodless bodies on the ground!

Dylan decided it was wise to get out of there and go home while everybody was focused out front. Nobody was aware of him leaving as he slipped away.

He could hear sirens blasting as he crossed the graveyard and opened the door to his house.

His parents looked up as he came in smiling.

"I see you had a good time," said his mother.

"And you did a little necking, I guess," said his father.

Dylan grinned and licked his lips. He thought of the fresh, drained bodies of the couple he had left in the courtyard.

"You know," he said to his parents, "covering my fangs and going as a boy was the best costume idea I ever had."

"That's nice," said his mother. "Maybe you can do it again next year!"

The Dead of Winter

"Do we have to stay at Grandma's house all winter?" Grace Lang asked her parents.

"No, honey," her father answered. "We're going to attend her funeral and then stay on two or three weeks to clear out the house and get her affairs in order."

"Why can't somebody else do that after the funeral?" asked Grace.

"Because I'm her only child," said Mr. Lang. "The house belongs to us now, so I want to get it ready to sell."

"I don't like living in the country," said Grace. "I want to stay at our house so I can do things with my friends."

Grace's parents, Maya and Thai, didn't like living in the country either, but Mr. Lang didn't want Grace to know. He had to try to keep up her spirits.

"It won't be long," said Mrs. Lang. "Besides, there are lots of things to do in the country, even in the dead of winter. You'll make some new friends while you are down in the country."

"What about school?" asked Grace.

"I talked to the principal, and she suggested that we home school you until we get back to the city. You've always been on the honor roll, and the teachers showed me what material they would cover while you're away. I filled out all of the necessary forms, so it won't be a problem," her mother explained reassuringly.

Grace slumped in her chair and looked very disappointed. She didn't want to go to the country. She didn't want to be home schooled. She wanted to be with her friends. A feeling of dread hung onto her like some desperate living thing, and she just couldn't shake it off.

She had never been to a funeral before, and she didn't know what to expect. Grandma Lang had never seemed sick to Grace when they visited her, but her mom said that she had died suddenly of a heart attack. Finally, the family was all packed and ready to go say goodbye.

The clouds looked dark and angry and seemed to hang especially low as the family left the city behind them. Grace decided the best thing to do was to take a nap, so she slept until they pulled into the drive at her grandmother's house.

Mrs. Cohen and her daughter Rebecca, who lived two doors down the road, were there to greet them. Grandma Lang and Mrs. Cohen had been close friends, and they kept keys to each other's houses. Grace and her parents had met them briefly when they came to visit Grandma Lang. Grace was happy that Rebecca was about her age.

Grandma Lang's body was already at the funeral home being prepared for the visitation that night. It would not be ready for viewing until seven o'clock.

"Come on in," said Mrs. Cohen. "I thought you might be hungry after the trip, so I've fixed some soup and sandwiches, and some hot coffee and hot cocoa to warm you up."

"That's very nice of you," said Grace's dad. "We really appreciate your handling things until we could get here."

"Yes," said Mrs. Lang. "I'm sure we will all feel better after we have had something hot to eat. The snow started just before we got here."

Rebecca and her mother joined them at the table.

"This has been such a shock to me," said Mrs. Cohen. "I don't know what I'll do without her."

"She never mentioned any health problems," said Mr. Lang. "Was something wrong that I didn't know about?"

"Well, there was just one thing that I thought was unusual," said Mrs. Cohen. "I probably shouldn't even mention it, but she complained of being cold all the time."

"That could have been an indication of her heart problem," said Mrs. Lang. "Poor circulation, you know."

"I suppose it might have been," said Mrs. Cohen, "but I think there was more to it. I know this sounds crazy since your mother was never afraid of anything, Thai, but I believe that she saw something out there in the dark that spooked her."

"My mother? Spooked?" laughed Mr. Lang. "I can't imagine such a thing."

"She said something strange to me one time," said Rebecca.

"What did she say?" asked Grace.

"Well, it was nearly dark, and she was out on her porch. She saw me walking up the road, and she walked down to meet me. She told me that the dead could walk about on winter nights, so I had better hurry home before the real dark came. She said I would never want to meet a dead person walking."

"Oh, my," said Mr. Lang. "That doesn't sound like her. Maybe I should have checked on her more often. Maybe she had circulation issues that were affecting her mind."

"She always sounded all right on the phone," said Mrs. Lang.

"Yes, she sounded good to me, too," agreed Mr. Lang.

"Mr. Lang," said Rebecca, "she might have heard about what happened here a hundred years ago. Some old tales can weigh on your mind."

"What happened?" asked Grace.

"Mom tells it better than I do," said Rebecca. "Tell them what happened, Mom!"

"Honey," replied Mrs. Cohen. "This might not be a very good time."

"No, please go ahead," said Mrs. Lang.

"A hundred years ago, there were no paved roads around here," said Mrs. Cohen. "The town's cemetery sat on top of that small hill over there. If someone died, the body was hauled up the hill to the cemetery by a wagon and mules. Of course, the winter snows sometimes made it impossible. They started up the hill with the corpse of an old woman, Mrs. Charity Flanagan, who had lived at the foot of the hill, but a foot of snow had fallen during the night.

"The mule team pulled and strained, but the wagon stuck in a snow drift about halfway up the hill. There was nothing to do but postpone the funeral until they could get the coffin up the hill to the cemetery. They left the corpse in her coffin on the wagon and led the mules back to the barn.

"It turned out that they had to leave the corpse there for six weeks. They finally got the grave dug and the body buried in the first row in the second plot. Now that much is proven fact. But I'm not sure about the truth of the rest of the story."

"Tell us anyway," insisted Grace.

"The story goes that during the six weeks in the dead of winter, Mrs. Flanagan's spirit walks at night, watching out for others who might be in danger from the cold. The bad part is that anyone who sees her dies very soon afterward. I just wonder if your mother could have encountered something that frightened her," she said, looking at Mr. Lang.

Mr. Lang shrugged his shoulders, and Mrs. Cohen changed the subject.

"There will be a short time for the family's private viewing first," she said.

"Thanks," said Mrs. Lang. "You have been so helpful."

"Rebecca and I will help you unload your car, and then we'll go on home and get ready to go to the funeral home. We'll meet you there. Neighbors have filled the refrigerator with casseroles, ham, fried chicken, vegetable dishes, and lots of cakes and pies. You won't have to cook for a few days, maybe even a week."

They accepted Mrs. Cohen's offer and soon had the car unloaded. Then they all got dressed for the visitation.

Grace held her breath as she and her family entered the funeral home. She saw her grandmother lying in a coffin at the front of a small chapel. She looked so out of place to Grace.

After they had viewed the corpse, her father spent extra time standing by the casket. Grace saw him wipe tears away as he left. She and her mother mingled with people she didn't know, because they had been friends of her grandmother. She was tired and relieved when the visitation finally ended and they were headed back to her grandmother's house.

As they walked from the car to the house, Grace felt someone was watching them. She could hardly wait for her mom to unlock the door. She pushed by and hurried inside.

"What's wrong with you tonight?" asked her mother.

"Nothing really," Grace answered. "But I felt like someone was watching us from the road. Then I thought I saw someone's shadow."

"Oh no!" said her father. "I hope we don't have a Peeping Tom out here!"

"I'm sure it was just the shadow of a tree limb," said Mrs. Lang.

She opened the door and looked up and down the road. There was nothing there. In fact, the snow had even stopped falling.

The next morning, it was a clear, cold day for the funeral. It seemed unreal to Grace to see the coffin lowered into the ground, knowing that Grandma Lang was in it. She dreamed about it that night and saw in her dream that Grandma Lang was very cold! Grace woke up so chilled that she was shaking.

That afternoon, Mrs. Cohen called and invited Grace to come play with Rebecca. Since her parents were busy going through papers and boxes that Grandma Lang had left behind, Grace was happy when they told her she could go. She grabbed her favorite stuffed animal, Moosie, and hurried down to Rebecca's house.

"Remember, dinner's at six," her mother called after her. "Be on time!"

Rebecca and Grace had such a good time playing that they forgot about the time. Mrs. Lang called to remind her daughter that she was late.

Grace jumped up, said goodbye to the Cohens, and ran all the way home.

Grace had not noticed until she was running down the road toward home that large snowflakes had started coming down thick and heavy. They were sticking and building up everywhere they fell.

Her mom was not happy that she was late for dinner, and Grace was not happy when her mother sent her to her room as punishment right after dinner. Without her phone to text her friends, Grace sat on the window seat and watched the snow accumulate. It looked like white sheets covering the dead in the morgue in scary movies.

She left the window and read until her father knocked on her door and told her it was time for bed.

Her parents went to bed soon after they tucked in Grace for the night. Soon the house was quiet and everything was still, but Grace couldn't sleep for some reason. Then she remembered.

She didn't have her stuffed moose with her. She had left it on the bench outside on the porch when they went out to see Rebecca's playhouse. It was still there, and Grace was certain the snow would blow in and cover the moose. She would be in big trouble if she ruined Moosie! She had to go get him.

She slipped quietly by her parents' room and tiptoed to the front door. She put on her coat but couldn't find her hat.

It won't matter, she thought. *I'll only be gone for a few minutes.*

It was a good thing that Rebecca's house was so close. Grace could barely see the road now, buried under all the snow. It was definitely colder now than when she had been out earlier.

She reached the Cohens' house and crept up the porch steps. Moosie was still on the bench, but the snow had not quite reached it yet. She grabbed it and carefully descended the steps into the yard. Then she hurried through the snow to the road as fast as she could. The wind picked up, and Grace felt like her ears were frozen. She wished she had taken time to find her hat.

She lowered her head, clutched Moosie, and struggled forward against the wind. She suddenly stopped because she had almost collided with an old woman in the road!

"Oh!" she exclaimed.

"Sorry, child," said the old woman. "I didn't mean to scare you! What are you doing out in the cold?"

"I had to go get my moose," said Grace. "I forgot it when I was at Rebecca's house today. You won't tell, will you? My mom and dad would be angry with me."

"No, I won't tell," said the old woman, "but you've got to get in out of the cold right now! You are not dressed properly. Where's your hat?"

"I couldn't find it, and I had to get my moose right away," Grace answered. "I'll be on my way now before my mom and dad know I'm gone."

"Here, child, put on my shawl," said the old woman. "It will cover your head nicely."

The old woman draped it over Grace's head and around her shoulders. Grace began to feel much warmer.

"Do you live around here?" asked Grace.

"I'm from down the road," she said. "I walked down to the house beyond yours tonight, and now I am on my way back."

"I thought I saw someone in the road one night," said Grace. "Maybe it was you out walking."

"Could have been," the old woman answered.

"I've really got to go," said Grace. "I hate to take your pretty shawl. How will I get it back to you?"

The old woman smiled.

"Just leave it on my grave in the morning," she said. "It's in the cemetery on the hill, first row, second plot!"

Without further comment, the old woman vanished in the cold, snowy night.

Grace clutched her moose tightly, but she could not make herself move. The snow blew around her, and she sank to the road, numb and exhausted. The white sheet of snow silently covered the dead.

"Thai, come quickly!" shouted Mrs. Lang. "Grace is not in her room, and Moosie's gone, too!"

They searched the house and the yard. Mrs. Lang called the Cohens, but they hadn't seen her since dinnertime. Mr. Lang called the police to report his daughter missing.

Mr. and Mrs. Lang put on boots, coats, hats, and gloves, and were ready to join the search when the police and some neighbors arrived. They searched along the road first but found nothing.

"Let's go up the hill," said the police officer. "Some kids are fascinated by the old cemetery. Sometimes they wander up there."

The search party followed the police up the road and entered the cemetery.

"Look!" the police sergeant shouted. "There's something in the first row."

They all rushed to the second grave in row one. The sergeant leaned down and picked up something. It was Grace's moose wrapped in a shawl!

No footprints led to or from the grave. If there had been any, the heavy snowfall last night would have covered them.

Weeks of looking for Grace turned up nothing, and, eventually, the police called off the search. The Langs never knew what happened to their daughter, and nobody ever thought of digging up the second grave in the first row in the dead of winter.

Excursions

I saw it first when I was driving to work one morning along River Road. It was a hot August morning, and the sun was already warning of even higher temperatures later in the day. There had been no forecast of fog, but there it was, rolling on top of the river right beside me.

That's odd, I thought. *I've never seen fog keep to the river like that. It usually covers the road.*

Since I was driving and having to watch the road, I had to satisfy my curiosity with side glances. Then I saw it! It was a face in the fog—a woman's face wearing a captain's hat. I must be imaging things!

I had to stop at a red light, so I had time to look straight at the fog. The face was still there. I could see it clearly! Hidden back in the fog was a dark form like one of those old excursion boats that used to travel the river. Impossible! Those boats weren't running anymore.

The light changed, and I drove on. The face in the fog continued to look at me until I turned left and headed away from the river.

I tried to put it out of my mind. Maybe it was a one-time happening. Maybe I had imagined the whole thing.

The next morning, I took my usual route to work along River Road. The sky was clear and the morning already hot when suddenly the fog appeared again. Again, when I glanced at it, I saw the same face and dark form in the water.

The driver in front of me must have seen it, too, because he suddenly slammed on his brakes and leaned to look toward the river. I slammed on my brakes and avoided hitting him by inches. I don't think he ever realized what a close call we'd just had. He straightened up, shook his head, and drove off without looking back.

I drove on to work wondering what was going on out there on the river. I was sure the river held more than its share of mysteries.

Every day that week, I began to feel very nervous as I approached the fog area on River Road. The urge grew stronger every day for me to stop and walk to the water's edge. Fortunately, my good sense prevented me from doing that.

One day, the traffic was at a crawl because of an accident up ahead. As luck would have it, I had to stop beside the face in the fog. I saw the head nodding, indicating that I should come join her. I looked the other way, but I could feel her staring at me. Fortunately, the traffic problem cleared, and I drove away as quickly as I could.

I tried to find another route to work, but anything I considered was longer and more congested. I would have to keep going by the stretch of fog.

It occurred to me while I was driving home one day that there might be a story behind this eerie happening. Maybe if I could find out what happened here, I could understand and maybe get rid of this apparition.

I searched online but did not find any specific explanation. Then I had more luck when I found some references from archived copies of old newspaper stories. After searching different topics, I finally found a story about an excursion boat tragedy.

Captain Summers was a greedy woman who made every effort to take a group out on the river every night on her excursion boat, *The River Queen*. One night, in a thick fog, she collided with a barge.

Nobody ever explained what happened, but there was an explosion on *The River Queen*, and everyone on board perished. Not all of the bodies were recovered, including the body of Captain Summers. There was not enough left of the boat to justify spending money to salvage it.

The article showed a picture of Captain Summers, and I had to admit she looked like the face in the fog!

The story made good spooky reading, but it wasn't something I could go out and talk about. If I told people that I had seen the face of the late captain of an excursion boat, and perhaps saw the ghostly form of the boat itself, I might have to undergo psychiatric evaluation just to keep my job.

It stayed on my mind all the time. Why had she come back to haunt the river? Had she been unable to contain her greed any longer and come to find passengers for her boat again?

I shuddered every workday when I had to drive by. I knew I had to do something to get away from the fog. I put in for a transfer to one of our offices across town. Then I waited.

One morning, I was driving to work when the face in the fog appeared as usual. The fog revealed the head and the arms that day. Captain Summers must be gaining strength to materialize more clearly.

The traffic had slowed, and I glanced over toward the river to see what was happening. Captain Summers looked right at me and motioned to me. The dark boat form was in the background. She wanted me to come aboard. No way was that going to happen!

The traffic moved ahead, and just as I started to accelerate and follow, a boy dashed in front of my car. I felt a thump, and the boy disappeared!

I pulled off into the grass by the riverbank and got out of my car to see if the boy was hurt. My car was only starting to move, so he probably wouldn't be seriously injured. Still, I wanted to be sure.

"Where are you?" I called out. "Are you hurt?"

I couldn't see him until he suddenly ran out of the fog that had crept to the bank now, and he stood facing me.

"Wait your turn, lady," he called out. "I'm going on the boat this trip!"

"No!" I cried. "Stop!"

The boy was already running toward Captain Summers. The fog opened up for the first time. I could see Captain Summers standing on deck with her arms stretched out. The boy ran toward the captain, and the captain reached out her hands and pulled the boy on board. The fog closed in immediately, and they were gone.

I didn't know what to do. I decided I had to notify the authorities. They might be able to rescue the boy.

The police took my statement, but I could tell that they only believed part of my story. They thought I was some hysterical female who didn't have her facts straight. They pieced together a report that satisfied them.

They said the boy fell into the water and that some people had rescued him. That was not the truth at all. The police filed the report and never followed up. That's why I am telling this story now. I hope someone will reopen the case and find out what really happened to the boy.

I don't see the fog and what it holds anymore, because I don't drive on River Road anymore. My transfer came through, and I moved out of the city to be closer to my work.

I still read the paper and listen to the news, though. I look for a story about a drowned boy, but none of them match what I saw.

I do see other stories of people drowning in that strip on River Road, though. I wonder if they are ordinary deaths or if they took their last trip on an excursion boat called *The River Queen*.

Grave Situation

I don't live in Fairmont anymore. I had to leave under sad circumstances. A car wreck wiped out all of my family, so I had no choice but to move. I couldn't live there with the guilt. You see, I was the one driving the car that night.

I realize you may not be listening to me at all. Some people tune me out like I'm not there. Maybe they don't want to listen to anything about death because it makes them think of their own mortality. I need to talk about it, though, because I need to understand why this happened so I can move on.

I had just celebrated my eighteenth birthday! My graduation present was a new car—well, new to me anyway. My parents had worked hard to save enough money to buy a used car for me. They knew I would need it next fall to drive to the community college nearby. I promised them and my little brother the first ride. We all climbed in and headed for the school to see the senior play. I was the stage manager, and I felt very proud of my responsibility for the production.

A light rain had set in about suppertime, so the roads were wet and slick. I was being extra careful until I got a text message from the lead actress (my best friend) in the play.

Normally, I would not text while driving. It's just too dangerous, and besides, it's against the law! I would not have answered it, but it crossed my mind that she might need me to stop and get something along the way. I should have pulled over, but I was giddy from the excitement of the new car and the play, so I didn't think about the possible consequences. I only looked away from the road for a few seconds. What could possibly happen in a few seconds?

In those few seconds, an eighteen-wheel tractor-trailer came barreling down the road from the opposite direction. Later, I realized it wasn't really speeding. It just looked like it was when I looked up and saw it coming right at us. My mind froze.

What was the truck doing on my side of the road?

My mother screamed the loudest scream I've ever heard. "Watch out!"

Then I realized I was the one on the wrong side of the road. I swerved away from the oncoming truck, but it was too late. The sound of the impact and screeching metal was horrific. I knew immediately that the crash was deadly. My car was thrown against a tree at the side of the road, and I sat reeling with the knowledge that I had just killed my parents and little brother.

Police cars, ambulances, and fire trucks arrived with sirens shrieking. The firemen had to use the Jaws of Life to remove us from the twisted metal. I saw the truck driver talking to the police before they took us away. At least I hadn't killed him.

The newspaper called the wreck the worst accident in the history of Fairmont. The senior play was cancelled that night. The townspeople talked of nothing else but the crash for weeks.

It turned out that I did a foolish thing by texting. My best friend had only wanted to tell me how cool my car was. That was the important text I risked my family's lives to answer. I could tell she felt guilty, but it wasn't her fault. She hadn't known I was driving when she sent it, and she hadn't known I would be foolish enough to try and answer it while I was driving.

Two days later, the town gathered for the multiple funerals of my family. The minister said, "Go in peace." I knew there would be no peace for me.

Afterwards, I could no longer live in our home and had to move, but I kept going back to Fairmont because I was drawn to the crash site. When I was there, my mind brought my family back to life for just a little while. I made myself walk down the familiar streets. Some people seemed unaware of me and walked by without speaking. A few people recognized me but hurried away, white-faced and frightened. They acted like I was some kind of monster that might wipe them out.

Our house had been sold, but I could still see my father getting his golf clubs out of the garage on Saturday mornings. He also loved to fish and had taught my brother and me how to catch, clean, and cook the fish we caught.

I remembered playing catch with my little brother. I had taken that joy away from him, and it would haunt me forever.

I saw my mother's garden. She often had me pick flowers with her to take to graves in the local cemetery where other relatives and close family friends lay buried.

These memories were going to be my ghosts, not white, shimmering figures in the night but thoughts that would continue to haunt me. Somehow I had to lay them to rest. Maybe someone would show me the light.

This morning, I would walk around for the last time and then try to move on. I was stiff at first, but I felt better as I walked along. There was a chill in the air, and I shivered as I walked past all the places I had loved.

I stood outside the high school, and suddenly I felt compelled to go inside. It was break time between classes when I stepped into the hall. Students ran past me to their classrooms without even looking at me.

Was I always in a hurry like that? I wondered.

It is astounding how one second can change your life forever. With one action, you can make a mistake that you can never take back. I knew that my punishment was that I was destined to relive what I had done forever. I could never go back to the way I was before the accident.

I left the school and walked down the road. I had never felt so alone. I came to the little cemetery outside of town. I saw a woman in the back putting flowers on a grave. The sight of her reminded me that I should put flowers on the graves of my mom, dad, and brother.

As I entered the cemetery, the woman stood up and walked across a grave. I shivered as I watched her go.

My mother used to say, "Someone's walking on my grave!"

I felt exactly that way now. I looked down, and I was standing on a grave! I looked at the headstone and read a familiar name.

"Good heavens!" I said to myself. "*Someone is walking* on *my grave*—and it's me!"

Then it hit me: I don't live in Fairmont anymore. I'm buried there!

The Bookworm

Lucy and Evelyn Chiu raced ahead of their father as they headed for the bookstore in the mall. Many of the stores closed at six o'clock, but the bookstore would be open until nine for tonight's special program.

Mr. Chiu wondered if the coming storm would affect attendance. He thought of staying home, but he didn't want to disappoint his daughters.

Lucy and Evelyn could hardly wait. Their favorite author, B. W. Crawley, was signing her new book tonight. She was also going to have some of her older books on hand, too, and Mr. Chiu had told the girls that they could buy the new one plus an older one. It was definitely going to be an evening the girls would never forget!

"Let's hurry! We should get a seat up front," said Lucy.

Evelyn and Mr. Chiu agreed, so they hurried into the bookstore and found seats in the front row. One old lady was already seated there, and she looked the three newcomers over as they sat down.

"I didn't think grownups liked B. W. Crawley's books," Lucy whispered to her father.

The old lady overheard and smiled.

"I have all of her books," said the old lady. "There is something about her writing that fascinates me. I guess I will always be a child at heart."

"Which of her books do you like best?" asked Lucy.

"*Bookworms*," said the old lady. "Of course, I haven't read her new one yet."

"We are going to buy her new book tonight," said Evelyn. "Dad said we could buy an older one, too."

"Let's buy *Bookworms*," said Lucy. "We don't have that one, do we, Dad?"

"No," said Mr. Chiu. "I would remember that title because you two are such bookworms. Why don't you get the two books you want, and I'll pay for them now. Then you'll be all set to get her to sign your books."

The girls brought the books to their dad, and he paid just as the program started.

B. W. Crawley started the program with some details about herself and her writing.

"I have always been a bookworm," she said. "You can usually find me in a bookstore or a library."

B.W. Crawley told some stories from her book, and then it was time for the autograph session. The old lady was first in line, followed by Lucy and Evelyn. The girls wanted their pictures taken with the author, so B. W. told them to stay until she finished signing and she would pose with them. The old lady waited, too.

Mr. Chiu was sure he had heard thunder near the end of the talk. He felt like leaving now, but the girls would be upset if they didn't have their pictures taken with their favorite author. He hoped the storm would pass quickly while they were inside.

B. W. Crawley graciously posed with the old lady and then the girls. The bookstore manager began closing up, so the old lady, Mr. Chiu and his daughters, and several other people left the store and headed to the front entrance. Two security guards followed them to lock up as soon as they left.

Mr. Chiu looked out and wished that he had followed his hunch to leave. The storm outside was raging, and anything loose on the ground was being hurled through the air. They would be soaked if they dashed for their car in the parking lot. Everyone stopped and watched the fury of the storm.

"Come on, people," said the security guards. "Everybody out! We have to lock up now."

They attempted to herd the people out the door, but nobody budged. One guard approached the old lady. He thought the rest would follow if he could get her to move.

"Come on, ma'am," he said. "We've got to close up the mall."

As he reached for her arm, the thunder boomed and lightning streaked across the sky. Raindrops tumbled over each other to hit the pavement.

"The only way I am going out in this storm," said the old lady, "is if you carry me!"

The small group of people moved in a bit closer to see how the security guards were going to handle this situation.

"We can't literally carry an old woman out into a storm," said one guard.

"Well," said the other, "we can't lock them up in the mall, either. What do you suggest?"

The first guard took charge.

"Ok, folks," he said, "we're going to lock up the rest of the mall and then come back here. The storm seems to be slacking off, so it should be over by the time we get back."

"Good," said the old lady. "We'll be here."

As the guards walked off, a man from the group said to the old lady, "I'm glad you spoke up. I didn't want to go out in the storm, either."

Another loud boom of thunder and forked lightning confirmed their good judgment in waiting out the storm inside the mall. But, of course, thunder and lightning have no brains and could not know what was to come.

The group by the mall entrance watched the guards disappear around the corner, and with the guards' presence removed, the mall took on a silent, spooky atmosphere. Shadows loomed larger than life, and the air inside felt charged with electricity as well as the outside where the storm was still strong and steady.

"Did Miss Crawley ever come out of the bookstore?" asked someone in the back of the group.

"I am sure they must have taken her out a private way," answered another.

"Or maybe she is waiting out the storm in the manager's office," said a third.

No one else spoke, and silence reigned.

The guards on the other side of the mall hurried to lock up and get back to the entrance.

"Is it just me, or does the mall seem especially creepy tonight?" asked the first guard.

"No, I feel it, too," said the second. "I guess it's the storm and the scary stories that writer read."

They both picked up the pace and turned the corner back toward the entrance.

The group moved closer together at the front door. One couple decided to make a run for their car, and they ducked their heads and dashed out to the parking lot. The ones inside watched as their car lights came on and they pulled out of the lot onto the street. Mr. Chiu debated in his mind whether to do the same. Lucy and Evelyn were huddled together, frightened, so he decided to stay. It was the last decision he would ever make.

It all happened at once. The storm calmed, and a gentle rain replaced the sheets that had violently covered the parking lot only a few moments before. The area inside the mall was dim with only the emergency lights on. The group heard a door opening behind them. They turned around and saw a long, white creature emerge, crawling from the bookstore.

It moved remarkably quickly and was on them before they could move. This monstrous, worm-like creature had a familiar face, and it smiled as it opened its mouth. They tried to move, but it was too fast for them. One after another, it sucked them all down its throat. The last thing Mr. Chiu remembered was the face of B. W. Crawley as she told the bookstore audience that she had always been a bookworm!

Its hunger satisfied, the creature pushed open the door and crawled to its car. Its transformation to a writer again would be soon, so it decided to go to the library and wait until it was hungry again. The guards heard a commotion and hurried around the corner. Everyone was gone!

They followed a slimy trail from the bookstore to the door.

That's odd, they thought. *Where could they all have gone? There's not a person in sight, and their cars are still here!*

The cars sat empty in the parking lot. Neither of the guards would ever know that B. W. Crawley's stomach was full.

Bag of Treats

Harry McSweeny loved Halloween more than any other holiday. Every year, he pestered his dad to make him a new costume, and he did it for him because it pleased Harry so much. He or Harry's mother would take Harry and his friends trick or treating every year.

After they had gone to all the houses in the neighborhood, Harry and his friends would come back to Harry's house and dump all their treats on the living room carpet to see what goodies they had. Sometimes they traded, but most of the time, they picked out a few treats to eat with the apple cider that Harry's mom provided.

"Why do you want a new costume every year?" asked one of his friends. "Nobody is going to remember what you wore last year."

"I don't want the Shadow Man to remember me," said Harry. "I have to trick him every year so he won't know me."

"Aw, come on, Harry," said another friend. "There is no such thing as a Shadow Man."

Harry would smile and pretend he was kidding, but he knew there really was a Shadow Man, because he often saw him. But he didn't say any more about him while his friends were there.

His friends went home, and another Halloween was history! Harry was happy that once more he had escaped. Nonetheless, Harry had problems going to sleep at bedtime. He was afraid the Shadow Man would come and take him away.

"I am going to try to find out where the Shadow Man lives," Harry said to himself. "If I find out, I can be sure to stay away from him."

Winter, spring, and summer came and went. School started in the fall, and Harry and his friends enjoyed every season. Nothing, though, was ever as much fun as Halloween.

Harry began looking at costumes in September.

"I want to go as the sun this year," Harry told his father.

"The sun?" he said. "Why do you want to be the sun?"

"Because the sun drives the shadows away," Harry told him.

"I am glad you decided early," he told him. "I'll have plenty of time to make it before Halloween."

While his father made the costume, he thought about Harry's fear of shadows. He tried to remember when it started, but it was too far back in Harry's past for him to recall details. He thought Harry had been frightened in a storm when the wind whipped the tree limbs around outside his window. This fear was beginning to become a significant problem for Harry. Maybe he would talk to his wife, and they could ask the counselor at school for a recommendation of someone to see.

Harry had a special request for this Halloween. He was especially helpful and responsible before his favorite day. He wanted his parents to agree to what he was going to ask for.

"Mom and Dad," he began, "I want to do something different this Halloween. My friends and I have talked it over, and we'd like permission to go trick or treating by ourselves without any adults going along this year."

"Really?" said Mr. McSweeny. He looked at Mrs. McSweeny and asked, "What do you think?"

"I think we might have to reduce the territory a little bit, but if you and the group are willing to stay in the boundaries we set, it should work out fine," she said. "My friends and I were going out alone trick or treating when we were your age."

"Things weren't so bad back then," said Mr. McSweeny. "There wasn't much crime in those days."

"Other parents will be out with their children," Mrs. McSweeny replied. "I think it will be perfectly safe. We've never seen anything even remotely dangerous while we've been out, have we?"

"No," he said, "we haven't. Okay, Harry. We will set some rules and neighborhood boundaries. If you guys agree, then you may go without any adults!"

"Great!" exclaimed Harry, running to hug his parents. "You're the greatest!"

When Halloween arrived, Harry and his friends, all dressed in costumes, gathered in his living room.

Mr. McSweeny spoke first. He outlined the physical boundaries where they could go. It only included houses where they knew the owners.

Mrs. McSweeny gave them the rules.

"I think you guys know what I am going to say. Look both ways before crossing the street. Don't take any treats from strangers. Don't eat or drink anything until you get home and we check it."

"We promise," all the friends said together.

They were excited as they started their first trick or treat venture on their own. The first block was easy because they knew everyone who answered the door. Then, as they crossed the street to the next block, Harry saw a shadow near the streetlight.

"Wait," he whispered. "Something is following us. I saw a big shadow! It is carrying a huge bag!"

"Don't start your thing with the Shadow Man," one friend told him. "Shadows always look huge under streetlights."

"Come on," said the other friend. "Let's ring some more doorbells and get some more treats."

Harry didn't say anything else. He quietly walked behind his friends and watched the Shadow Man over his shoulder. As long as the shadowy thing kept its distance, he was okay.

They had reached the backside of their designated area now, and it was darker back here. The group looked around and checked their surroundings.

"Look!" said Harry. "There is a light in that old house over there. Nobody has lived in there for years."

"Maybe someone is throwing a party there tonight," said one of his friends. "It would be fun to rent a spooky place like that on Halloween."

The friends stood listening to kids up and down the street, laughing and screaming and enjoying the night. Then it got quiet. Their parents had probably called them inside.

The group watched the house for a few minutes. Then something came up toward the house.

"Look," said Harry. "There's the thing I told you was following us. Did you ever see such a big bag in your life?"

"No," said one friend. "He must be a giant to carry a bag like that!"

"What could he be carrying in a bag that big?" asked the other.

"He always looks hungry," said Harry. "Maybe he's looking for treats to eat!"

The group hid behind a hedge and watched the shadowy figure go up to the old house. As he approached, the door opened, and the kids couldn't believe their eyes.

"No!" said Harry.

"It can't be!" said one friend.

"He is pulling kids out of the big bag and feeding them to the little shadows!" said the other. "That guy at the door is their father!"

When the huge bag was empty, Shadow Man started out to fill it again.

"Let's follow him," said Harry.

"Are you nuts?" asked one friend.

"That's out of bounds for us," said the other.

"I'm going to follow him and see what he does," said Harry. "You guys do whatever you want."

Harry moved from behind the hedge, looked both ways, and crossed the street.

At least I obeyed Mom's rule about looking both ways, he thought.

His two friends hesitated a few seconds and then followed Harry. Much to their surprise, the Shadow Man was headed to their street! They heard voices again. The kids were still out-side playing after all. They did not see the Shadow Man creep-ing up behind them.

"Look out!" yelled Harry and his friends.

Their warning came too late! As the children turned to see what the yelling was all about, the Shadow Man opened his giant bag and brought it down over their heads. As he pulled it closed, he looked at Harry and his friends. They ran for home as fast as they could! The Shadow Man followed.

"Come inside," said Harry, when they made it to his house, but his two friends wanted to get to their own houses. Harry made it safely inside, while his friends kept running. Harry watched in horror from the window as the Shadow Man glided up behind them and brought the big bag down over their heads.

"NOOOOOO!" screamed Harry.

His parents rushed to see what was wrong, but Harry was too shocked to speak another word.

Harry allowed them to put him to bed and turn out all the lights. He welcomed the darkness.

No light, no shadows, he thought.

But he knew that the morning light would come, seasons would pass, and the Shadow Man would bring his bag back to look for more treats next Halloween.

Scaredy Cat

Ali was scared of everything. He always had been as long as he could remember. His sister, Kalie, just one year older, knew exactly how to set him off and make him run screaming to whichever parent was nearby. Kalie was afraid of some things, too, but she was smart enough to keep her fears to herself.

Ali could remember enough scary times to write a book, but he was afraid nobody would like it if he did. Even his mom and dad thought he was foolish.

"Ali," his dad would say, "go to the cellar and bring me up a quart of green beans."

"Dad, please send Kalie," begged Ali. "I'm afraid to go down there. Something is always in the cellar!"

Kalie would laugh and say, "Scaredy cat! Scaredy cat! I know where the monster's at! It's right behind you!"

Ali would whirl around, but instead of a monster, he would see his father scowling at him.

"Ali, I don't have time for your foolishness. You're just act-ing silly. Now, go get the beans!" his father ordered.

While Ali made another plea for his dad to send Kalie in-stead of him, Kalie snuck down the cellar steps and waited very quietly until Ali had grabbed the jar of beans from the shelf and started across the cellar toward the stairs. Then she stood up by the steps and said, "Ooooh!"

Ali dropped the jar of beans and bounded up the steps, two at a time. Kalie ran up behind him and escaped being seen because of all the commotion.

Ali was lectured about wasting food and was made to go down to the cellar and clean up the broken jar and the spilled beans. His father also sent him to bed without supper.

There were other times that things were just as bad. There was the time when the family went camping. Ali begged and pleaded not to go.

"There is always something in the woods!" said Ali. "I don't want to sleep in a tent. Something will get me!"

The minute he said that, Kalie started to think of how to scare her brother in the woods. "Scaredy cat! Scaredy cat! I know where the monster's at! It's . . ."

"Stop that, Kalie," said her mother. "You are scaring your brother. Now, Ali, you have nothing to be afraid of. We'll all be there together."

Kalie remembered she had a toy snake in her room. She slipped it in her duffle bag while she was packing. She didn't tease her brother anymore on the drive to the campsite.

Kalie and her mother set up the tent, which was large enough for the four of them. They unrolled their sleeping bags so they would be ready for bed. Kalie snuck into the tent, removed the snake from her duffle bag, and placed it in her own sleeping bag so she could easily reach it after they were all asleep.

After they ate the delicious food that their father had brought along, Ali and Kalie asked their mom to tell some stories around the campfire. Ali loved the stories because his mom usually told funny ones, but tonight she told a scary one that made Ali move as close to his dad as possible. He stayed there until it was time for them to go to bed.

Ali insisted that his dad sleep next to the tent flap so he could keep anything from coming through the door. His mom's sleeping bag was next, then his, and then Kalie's bag.

His mom and dad fell asleep immediately. Kalie pretended to be asleep, but she was only waiting until Ali dozed off. He had trouble going to sleep, though, because he kept thinking of monsters in the woods. Finally, sleep conquered him!

Kalie eased the toy snake out of the bag and gently placed it inside Ali's sleeping bag. Then she shook his bag just enough to wake him. When he sat up, he felt the toy snake—and Kalie got the exact reaction she had hoped for.

"Eeeek! Eeeek! Eeeek!" he screamed.

Kalie had never seen anyone come out of a sleeping bag so fast. Now Ali was stomping on the bag and throwing his hands in the air. Just as Kalie had hoped, he hit the tent poles, and the tent collapsed on the four of them. During the uproar, Kalie picked up the toy snake and put it back in her own sleeping bag out of sight.

The trip was ruined. The family cut it short, packed up the next morning, and drove home.

"Ali," said his father. "I think it is time we got you some professional help. Your fear of everything is totally unreasonable."

Ali didn't object. He wanted to be rid of these extreme fears that continued to plague him.

His father made an appointment for him with Dr. Jane Maxwell for the next week. He was a little scared of going, but he liked Dr. Maxwell at first sight.

After the introductions, Dr. Maxwell got right down to business.

"Before you can deal with a fear," she said, "you have to identify it. You have to give it a name. For instance, I once had a patient who was afraid to fly. As we sorted through the different names she put on her fear, it turned out that what she was really afraid of was the loss of control. She had to trust her life to the pilot flying the plane."

With each session, Ali saw more clearly that he had to deal with one fear at a time. He had to name it, confront it, and decide what he had to do to deal with it. He was sixteen now and ready to conquer the world.

When he finished his sessions with Dr. Maxwell, Ali felt confident that he was now in control of his phobias. Kalie had lost interest in playing tricks on him, so he was lulled into a false sense of security.

The first thing he did was to get his driver's license. He hadn't tossed fearfully the night before with fear and self-doubt. He marched into the license division, took the test, and passed.

Fear no longer intruded on his daily life, but on one summer day, it was waiting for one last chance.

Ali had driven to his friend's house for his birthday party. The party began at 2:00 p.m. so he had plenty of time to drive home before dark. His parents liked for him to be home while it was still light until he had more driving experience.

The party was a success, and Ali had a wonderful time. He was getting ready to head home when he heard a rumble of thunder.

Oh, no, he thought. *I've never driven in a storm. I had better hurry home before the storm hits.*

Ali said goodbye to his friends and those remaining at the party. As he pulled out of the driveway, he realized the dark clouds were approaching more quickly than he had thought.

It was too late to change things now, though. He was already out on the road, and he didn't want to go back to his friend's house. From the looks of the clouds, it might rain all night. He quickly decided that it would be better to drive in the storm while it was still daylight than to try to drive in the dark with pouring rain.

He had gone about seven miles when his engine started to sputter. He only had enough time to steer his car to the shoulder of the road before it died completely.

"What could be wrong?" he asked himself. "Mom just had it checked out last week, and everything was fine."

Then he remembered his dad had told him to fill up the car with gas before he left, but he had forgotten to do that. He looked at the gas gauge, and it confirmed his problem. The gauge was registering empty.

Ali tried calling home, but he couldn't get a signal on his cell phone. The storm must be interfering. He tried to think of what to do next. He began to panic.

"Now, calm down. There is a solution to this problem. I just have to figure it out," he told himself. "What would Dr. Maxwell tell me to do?"

Thunder rolled in closer. Lightning was close behind. He thought he still had a few minutes left before it started to rain.

Ali looked at his surroundings for the first time. There was an old house! Maybe they had a landline phone that worked. He could take shelter there and ask if they would let him call home.

Ali checked to see that all of his car windows were rolled up and locked the car doors. Then he dashed to the house.

He knocked on the front door, but he could tell right away that no one was home. The porch was littered with leaves and twigs, and the mailbox was stuffed with weatherworn ads and junk mail. He shook the door, thinking he might be able to get inside for shelter, at least. He ran to the back door, but it was locked, too.

The wind had picked up, and Ali was struggling to stand against it. He was terrified now that he realized the storm was going to catch him. He looked for some place to go. The car was too far away, but he spotted a barn beyond the backyard.

Ali ran as quickly as he could. His lungs burned, aching from lack of oxygen. He forced himself to keep moving, even though the eerie appearance of the barn looming ahead almost caused him to stop. It was not as frightening as the storm, though, so he doubled his efforts to outrun the rain. He made it to the barn as a clap of thunder sounded right behind him!

The barn door was partially open, so Ali pushed it ahead of him and ran inside. He barely made it when the storm broke! This was a bad one. Ali wished with all his being that he could be home with his family instead of here alone with a storm raging around him.

The barn was warm and stacked with bales of hay. Ali sat on the nearest bale and tried to catch his breath. He heard a low noise somewhere behind him and trembled. He thought immediately of his sister's words.

*Scaredy cat! Scaredy cat! I know where the monster's at....
It's behind you!*

With all his effort, Ali blotted her words from his mind! He couldn't blot out the storm, though. It came at him from all sides now. The rain peppered the roof like bullets. The wind sought out every crack and opening and forced its way inside, howling and blowing some of the straw around on the floor. The thunder shook the structure, and the lightning bolts came one after the other, striking so close that it made Ali tingle.

His fear grew at every sound and every lightning strike. He was totally irrational now. His fear was now in total control.

It is always in the barn, he thought. *The monster is always ....*

Then there was a lull in the storm, just long enough for Ali to hear the sound behind him again. Something was beside him. He could feel it.

Then the fur of the monster rubbed against his face. It had him. There was nothing he could do! Blood gushed through his body. His brain felt like it was going to explode. His heart was pounding.

But then he remembered his training. He breathed deeply and focused on taking deep breaths.

After several minutes, he slowly opened his eyes to see a barn cat. The barn cat that had rubbed against his face earlier looked puzzled. It flicked its tail, jumped over the bales, and snuggled down in the straw.

The storm continued, but the sound of the wind and the rain now felt soothing. The barn cat and Ali slept peacefully through the night.

The next day, after the storm, Ali's cell phone was working again, and he was able to call for roadside assistance. As they pulled his car away, however, he failed to turn around and notice the giant cat's eyes staring out at him from the dark windows of the house.

Better Not Mess with What's Best Left Alone

In the Sinkhole

Sinkholes are in the news a lot lately. People don't think about them most of the time, maybe because it is scary to think about the idea that the earth can open up without warning and swallow something as big as a house at anytime!

A sinkhole is an area of ground that has no natural external surface drainage. Rocks like limestone and salt beds under this land's surface are dissolved and eroded away to form holes. Florida, Kentucky, Missouri, Tennessee, and some western and midwestern states are prone to developing sinkholes over time. Fortunately, most sinkholes are small and cause no damage, but recently, several large sinkholes have caused serious problems.

One opened up in 2014 under the Corvette Museum in Bowling Green, Kentucky and swallowed up eight Corvettes. In 2015, another one that seemed only to like cars opened up at an IHOP in Meridian, Mississippi. There were twelve cars that went down in that one.

Nobody was hurt at either location, but that was because these particular sinkholes had no appetite for human beings. Julietta Flores knew that for a fact, even though scientific evidence did not support her theory. She knew that different sinkholes had appetites for different things because she had lived by a sinkhole when she was growing up, over sixty years ago.

She grew up on her family's farm way out in the country. There was a sinkhole close to the outhouse. Sometimes, she would hear a gurgling in the sinkhole when she and her sisters, Isabella and Amy, went to the outhouse at bedtime. Once when she was standing outside waiting for her sisters to finish, Julietta thought the sinkhole actually spoke to her.

"C-o-m-e," it seemed to say over and over.

"Hurry up, girls," she called, "or I am going to leave you!"

That threat usually motivated the two younger sisters to get a move on. If it didn't scare them into hurrying, Julietta's mom would yell from the back porch, "The monster in the sinkhole is coming up to get you if you don't come on!" Then the three of them would race to the house without looking back.

The girls did not like it when their father told them to take food scraps to the sinkhole. When they stood at the edge to dump the scraps in, they imagined that a giant tongue was about to reach out and slurp in the food. They always felt that if they stood there a second too long, it would slurp them in, too.

One day, when their Grandpa Hugo was there, he killed a chicken for dinner.

"Here, girls," he said. "Run and throw these chicken feet in the sinkhole. I don't want the dog dragging them around the yard, gnawing on them."

"Oh, Grandpa!" they wailed together.

"Go on now!" he ordered.

They obeyed, but they stood at a good distance and threw them in. As they ran back to the house, the sinkhole seemed to make a crunching sound. They were certain it was not their imagination!

Their grandpa only sighed and shook his head.

Then their cousin Oliver came to visit. He lived two farms over and came to play with the girls when he had nothing better to do. They all got along well, but Oliver wasn't convinced that there was a monster in the sinkhole.

Oliver threw a dead pigeon in once. A car had hit it, and he scraped it up and threw the whole thing in the sinkhole. The sinkhole made one of those gurgling sounds. It must have been pleased.

"It's got an appetite for flesh!" Julietta told him.

"Then don't get too close," he teased. "It might eat you!"

The girls often wondered just what might be down in that sinkhole. It had been there longer than they had been around. It could be a hiding place for bodies or anything!

They discussed it sometimes when the family was sitting on the front porch at night visiting with Oliver's family. Oliver thought there might even be some bodies left in there.

"Do you think the sinkhole was here when dinosaurs lived here?" Oliver asked his dad one night during one of these visits.

"I doubt it, but maybe," said his father.

"Mom," Julietta asked, "do you think there are any bodies in our sinkhole?"

"Of course not," said her mom. "Now stop talking about all this foolishness! It's only an old sinkhole that we put garbage in."

The sinkhole was put out of everybody's minds until Anna Noller came up missing. Wondering what happened to Anna pushed every other subject to the sidelines. The sheriff formed a posse, and they began searching the countryside for any sign of her.

Anna Noller was a girl whose mother had died and who had no supervision from her drunken father at home. Anna started out as a nice girl, but conditions at home eventually wore her down. Her father beat her on a regular basis, so Anna snuck out of the house when she could and hung out with her friends. These new friends were considered the wrong crowd by people who had nothing better to do than talk about it.

Of course, nobody would admit that they had seen Anna once she disappeared. Her father sobered up for a week, long enough to swear he hadn't seen her either. Since it was common knowledge that he had been abusive to Anna before, his word was questionable. There was no proof that he had harmed Anna in this instance, though, so the search continued.

Some people thought it was odd that Old Man Noller didn't join the search for his daughter. He didn't seem too concerned whether they found her or not.

It was Carter Locklear's old bloodhound, Sniffer, that finally found Anna—well, most of her anyway. She was in a clump of bushes near her house, but her head was no longer attached and it was nowhere to be found! And both of her hands were missing. They didn't find them either.

The town buried what they could find of her in a closed coffin. Old Man Noller was too drunk to show up at the funeral.

All the searching had come to a dead end when they had looked in every logical place.

That's when people started thinking about the sinkhole again. What a perfect place to hide body parts! Nobody would ever find them there, because there is really no good way to search a sinkhole.

Julietta, Isabella, and Amy took in every detail they heard and stored it in their heads for future use. They decided they would figure out who the killer was. Feelings were running high with a killer loose, and everybody was uneasy and on edge.

In the days that followed, Julietta began to feel something different now when she went near the sinkhole. Its appetite had changed. She couldn't explain it, but she knew. There was something different about the gurgling sounds. They sounded like something that had complete control.

She didn't dare mention the strange sounds, because even her own family would think she was crazy, but there was an order to what was happening in the sinkhole! Julietta finally told her sisters, and the three of them began to watch the sinkhole from Julietta's window when everyone else had gone to sleep. They had almost given up seeing anything when it happened.

It was a Saturday night. Old Man Noller had had way too many drinks at the pool hall and had bragged that nobody would ever solve his daughter's murder. He didn't actually confess with words, but his body language spoke the truth. He laughed and staggered around and then acted like he was cutting off her head and hands.

Arrests aren't made on body language alone, though, so Old Man Noller left the pool hall and started the long walk down the dark road to his house.

There was a hook moon in the sky that night, stingy as always with its light. Noller was too drunk to remember that a hook moon is supposed to be able to pull the dead from their graves. He staggered down the road feeling safe.

Back at the sinkhole, the hook moon had done its work. Something was rising from the depth of the sinkhole.

Every sound on the farm stopped. Something unearthly was happening. Danger was walking about.

Julietta, Isabella, and Amy sat watching that night. They knew the story of the hook moon, and they agreed that the little sliver of light in the sky might use its power tonight to bring justice to Anna Noller's murderer.

Midnight came, and the girls sensed the change in the atmosphere. The night was silent, but the air was charged with excitement. Nothing moved except the surface of the sinkhole. The girls could not take their eyes off of it as something splashed to the surface. For years, they could not speak of what they had seen that night without trembling.

The creature slowly made its way to the edge of the sinkhole. It climbed out awkwardly but finally succeeded and stood on wobbly legs. It began to walk but stopped in the backyard not far from the window where the girls were watching.

Even though the light was pale, they could make out the ghastly features. The head was definitely Anna Noller's. The body was made up of scraps melted together, and the hands were chicken feet with sharp claws. They were covering real hands, limp and broken! The spirit of the dead girl had built a body from the contents of the sinkhole and was off to seek revenge!

The girls held each other and watched as the awful thing walked slowly on shaky legs down the road in the direction Old Man Noller was coming. The girls had no idea where it was going at that point, and they didn't dare follow.

They huddled together until an hour or more had passed, and then they saw the thing come back! It waded into the sinkhole and sank beneath the calm surface. The three sisters looked at each other, and no one had the slightest idea of what they should do next.

Should they tell their parents? That was not a good idea. Their parents would scold them for being up after bedtime and tell them to stop talking nonsense.

Should they tell the kids at school? That was an even worse idea. The kids would laugh at them, and the teachers would think they were crazy.

Right then and there, they made a pact never to tell anyone what they had seen. After all, they had succeeded in their mission to solve the mystery of what was living in the sinkhole! All they had to do was stay as far from the sinkhole as possible. That wouldn't work too well, though, because of the location of the outhouse.

The next morning, they heard about what happened when the spirit met its killer! Old Man Noller was found ripped to shreds by the side of the road. There were no tracks, and there were no clues.

The sheriff was puzzled. It looked like a revenge killing to her, but there was no way, in her mind, that the ghost of Anna Noller could have come from her grave and killed her father. After discussing the matter with her deputy, the sheriff wrote it off as a wild animal attack.

Julietta and her sisters discussed it, and they decided that the sheriff was probably right. In a sense, they knew that the killer really was a wild animal!

When they went to the outhouse at night, they began to have concerns about whether or not that monster would stay down in the sinkhole. What if it had seen them watching from the window? What if it came out to get them? They simply had to talk to someone.

After some serious consideration, they decided to make some kind of tombstone since the sinkhole was Anna Noller's grave.

The next morning, Isabella and Amy spent time breaking green beans for their mother. Finally, they saw Julietta coming from the tool shed. They took the beans inside and ran to meet her.

"What do you think of this?" Julietta asked, presenting her creation.

It was a simple wooden cross. She had used her wood burning kit to write *R. I. P, Anna.* It couldn't have been better.

The girls ran down to the sinkhole, Amy said a prayer for Anna, and together, they gently threw the cross in.

Nothing happened for a couple of minutes, and then a strange gurgle came from the sinkhole. To the three girls waiting at the edge, it sounded like a thank you from Anna.

"Do you think she will come out again?" asked Isabella.

"No," said Julietta. "Let's leave her in peace."

They tried to do just that.

Life got back to the way it was before, except it wasn't long before the Flores family finally got an indoor bathroom!

Rest in Pieces

Brianna White lay sleeping peacefully until the *Chink! Chink!* on her coffin lid roused her. Who on earth was digging through six feet of dirt to disturb her rest? How dare they!

The chinking stopped and now she heard voices.

"What the heck is this?" asked a male voice.

Brianna wasn't sure, but it sounded like John Bradshaw. *Creep!* she thought. *Everyone in that family is a creep.*

"A coffin!" exclaimed another voice. "What's a coffin doing in this plot?"

There was no doubt about that second voice. It was David Kuramoto, the gravedigger.

"What am I supposed to do?" he asked.

"I have no idea!" John Bradshaw answered. "My family has owned this plot for years. No one is supposed to be buried here."

"That's a lie, and you know it!" Brianna White whispered in her coffin. "This land has always belonged to my family. My brother buried me here after I died, and then he went off and died himself before he could mark my grave. Your crooked old grandfather, Jim Bradshaw, grabbed our land and no one even looked for me. He said I'd gone off to live with relatives. Nobody bothered to check, because I was an old woman and no one really cared."

"I don't think your Grandfather Jim is going to be pleased to share his grave," said David. "What should we do?"

"I don't know," said John. "I don't want to report it to the authorities, that's for sure. I'd be tied up in red tape forever."

"Yeah," said David. "I see what you mean."

"I want to bury the old man as fast as I can," said John. "I want his estate settled right away."

John put his hand in his pocket and felt the handwritten will. He couldn't believe that his grandfather had changed his will and left everything to his cousin instead of him. John had done everything for his grandfather, and this was how his grandfather repaid him. No, it was not going to work like that! His grandfather was going to get what was coming to him.

"Well, what are you going to do?" asked David. "I have to have this grave ready by 10:00 a.m. tomorrow."

"Well, you're the gravedigger," said John. "How do you explain how this grave already has a body in it?"

"I can't," David answered. "We have no record of anyone being buried here."

"Ah," said John, "then if there is no record of anyone being buried here, we can remove this body and nobody will ever know. The grave will be empty for Grandfather Jim, right?"

"I don't know. Are you sure about that?" said David.

John was committed now and ignored David's question. This had to work. His grandfather had trusted him and had given him his last will to file.

Fat chance, old man! he thought. *You didn't think I would read it before I filed it, did you? Good thing for me that I did!*

No one else knew about the changed will, so he would keep it secret and keep the one that left him everything.

"Let's get started. Come on! Hurry!" John ordered.

Immediately, the digging began. When the coffin was completely uncovered, David stopped.

"You're going to have to help me get this coffin out of here," he said to John. "I'll get some ropes."

For the next few minutes, Brianna White was jostled about in her coffin. Then she was above ground.

"Are we going to see who's in here?" asked David.

"No," said John. "It doesn't matter anyway. Let's drag it over to the ledge and push it over."

Brianna White had to suffer the indignity of being moved. She had no choice. She could hear both men grunting as they struggled to move the coffin along. Then suddenly she was airborne, suspended only for seconds, and smashed against the ground. The coffin broke open, and Brianna's bones flew over the graveyard in pieces. The coffin slid on over the ledge out of sight. Brianna had to lie there for a while before thinking how to get herself together.

The two men picked up Brianna's bones and threw them in some bushes at the side of the graveyard. Then they went back to the grave, finished the digging, and prepared the plot for the burial of Grandfather Jim.

"Put my bones back!" she cried. "Put my bones back!"

The two men drove away from the graveyard without a glance back.

But death had not killed Brianna White's determination. She started about the business of putting herself back together. She found that she could roll her head about, so she would roll it along the graveyard fence when someone passed. She was not going to stop until she found a way to get John Bradshaw!

"Put my bones back!" she cried. "Put my bones back!"

People heard her and saw the rolling head, but nobody would admit it. It would be crazy to admit seeing something like that! Soon most people stopped walking by the graveyard.

Brianna didn't like being topside, exposed to all the elements, even if it did allow her to keep up with what was going on in the world. One day she heard that John was going to court to have the will probated.

The handwritten will was folded deep in John's coat pocket, well hidden. Soon he would be rich! Soon he would have his grandfather's money and be on his way out of town.

But Brianna White had other plans. As soon as the probating procedure started, Brianna entered the courtroom to get herself a piece of the action. Her white, bony hand crept unnoticed across the courtroom. It moved silently to John Bradshaw and crawled up his leg to his pocket. It gave a little tug to get his attention. John looked down and saw the white bones protruding out of his pocket.

John's eyes opened wider and wider!

"Put my bones back," a voice whispered.

"Get away! Get away!" he shouted.

The hand scratched him a little on the side from the pocket. He couldn't stand it. He suddenly began to scream and pull everything from his pocket. He threw the new handwritten will on the floor. The bony hand quickly slid down his leg and onto the floor. It moved under a chair, out of sight.

Chaos erupted as John continued screaming, "Get away! Get away!" The attorney stepped around him, picked up the handwritten will, read it, and handed it to the judge. The judge banged her gavel. Deputies led John away as he continued to scream.

When a voice said, "Put back my bones! Put back my bones!" the courtroom cleared with record speed.

Some serious investigations followed that memorable day in court. John's cousin received Grandpa's money. John Bradshaw was assigned to a residential facility for mentally ill criminals. David Kuramoto gave up his gravedigger job and started working for a landscaping company. DNA tests showed the white, bony hand belonged to Brianna White. With a little snooping around, the investigators learned the story of what had happened to her.

The townspeople declared a Brianna White Bone Day and went to the cemetery to find as many of her bones as they could. They buried what they found in a proper funeral. But they couldn't find all of her bones, so poor Brianna White still can't rest in pieces.

Her voice still calls from the graveyard at midnight in the mist, on stormy nights when there's a full moon.

"Put back my bones! Put back my bones!"

If you're brave enough to walk by the graveyard after a storm, on a misty night when there's a full moon, you may hear her calling. Those who know Brianna White say she won't give up until her last request is finally honored!

Hunters

Noah Reid and his friends were deer hunters, and they were as proud of shooting a deer as they would have been of shooting a bear. They were good, too! They never came home from a hunt empty-handed.

Noah's wife, Imani, did not approve of shooting defenseless animals, but she could accept it as long as the animal was used for food. She had to admit that the meat was tasty and that her husband didn't waste any of it.

What concerned her about the hunts lately was the way Noah had started acting. He came home each time now with a strange look in his eyes, a look of fear! When she asked him about it, he told her she was imagining things!

Noah and his friends were all set to head out for another hunt. Noah went to bed early the night before so he would feel rested and alert. Something kept him awake, though. He couldn't deny that Imani's questioning had upset him. He had been trying to ignore the uneasiness he experienced on hunts now, but she had made him face it.

He told himself over and over that killing deer was not a bad thing. They were over-populated and beginning to starve as they ran out of safe habitats. He and his friends were saving them from a slow, painful death. The ones that weren't killed would then have plenty to eat and would survive. He had always believed that. But why couldn't he believe it tonight? Maybe it was because of what happened at the beginning of the season with the doe.

He hadn't meant to shoot a doe! He thought he was firing at a buck, but the doe was suddenly in the line of fire. It was the oddest thing. She came from nowhere. She was dying when he got to her, but she had given him a look he had never been able to understand. All he knew was that it was not a look of forgiveness!

Tonight his fear and uneasiness persisted, and he could not go to sleep. He couldn't shake the feeling that he was being watched by something in the field and trees near the house. He couldn't resist the urge to get up, close the window, and lock it. He stood for a minute or two looking across his yard and garden, which stood between him and the trees.

It was dark, but flashes of lightning coming from gathering clouds gave enough light from time to time for him to see the tree line. His keen eyes saw movement among the trees.

The wind from the storm must be blowing the branches, he thought.

He had just about convinced himself that he had imagined the whole thing when he saw something again. It didn't really look like tree limbs blowing in the wind! A loud sound

came faintly from the woods. It sounded like many feet stomping, but it had to be low thunder.

"What's going on?" asked Imani, coming into the bedroom. "What are you doing up?"

She had decided to go to bed early, too, since the storm
sounded like it was going to be a rough one.

He didn't want to tell her there was something in the
woods that he couldn't explain.

"The thunder woke me," he lied. "I wanted to make sure
I had closed the window. I didn't want the rain to blow in."

He was relieved that he had a logical excuse to close the
bedroom window, since they usually slept with it open.

"Let's try to get some sleep," said Imani. "I want to sleep
through this storm. Bad weather makes me so nervous."

Noah slipped quickly into bed and lay very still so his wife
could sleep. It was an effort to keep from trembling as the storm
broke. He could still feel something moving about out there,
and he was not about to get up to go see what it was! He finally
drifted into a light sleep.

When the alarm went off in the morning, the storm
was over. Noah dressed and made some coffee as he
waited for his hunter friends to pick him up. He had a few
minutes left before his buddies were scheduled to arrive,
so he took his coffee and walked down to the tree line.
He looked closely at the ground, but all he saw were deer
tracks. That wasn't so unusual, except that there were so
many of them!

He made it back to the house just as his friends pulled
up. Soon the chatter and good spirits of his friends made him
feel a little foolish about being scared last night!

It was a successful day for the hunters. Each one bagged a deer, and each felt very proud of what they had done. They laughed, joked, and sang old songs from their youth all the way home.

Noah gulped down his dinner and went outside to clean the carcass. But the whole time, he felt uneasy, like something or someone was watching him from the trees.

I need a good night's sleep to throw this off, he thought. *Then everything will be back to normal again.*

When he finished cleaning the carcass, he took a hot shower and told Imani he was going to bed. He was so tired; he knew he would sleep soundly tonight. He was right. He was asleep as soon as his head hit the pillow.

Imani was careful not to wake him when she came to bed. She, too, slept soundly because she had not rested well last night on account of the storm.

Imani awoke to Noah's screams. His arms were over his face like he was trying to protect himself, but Imani saw nothing.

He must be having a terrible dream, she thought.

"Noah! Wake up!" she said.

Noah could barely hear her voice. He could not respond. The dream held him captive. He felt each hoof pounding him as the endless stream of deer ran over his body, pounding him without mercy. The sound of the pounding was roaring in his ears!

Imani heard nothing but his screams. She ran and dialed 911 for help, but by the time EMS arrived, Noah wasn't breathing.

She waited at the hospital until the doctor finished examining Noah. When Imani saw the doctor come out to talk to her, she knew Noah was dead.

"What happened?" she asked.

"To be absolutely truthful, I can't explain it." The doctor paused. "His body is covered with hoof prints like he was trampled to death in some kind of stampede! But the really odd thing is that the hoof prints look like they came from deer."

Time Capsule

The Workman family was used to moving, so Gabriel and Emma were not upset when their father, an army colonel, was transferred to a new post. Nicolas and Antonia were grateful that their children adapted so well to change. They expected nothing unusual to happen here. So much for expectations!

It would be three weeks before school started, so the twins would have plenty of time to settle in and explore their surroundings.

There was a welcoming party at the base, so they met families and children who would attend school with Gabriel and Emma. Kimi and Ben Tang, two kids who would be Gabriel and Emma's classmates, lived on the same street, and they offered to show Gabriel and Emma around town the next day. Of course, Gabriel and Emma were happy to accept. Everything was going along as usual so far.

It was clear and hot the next day, but the children paid little attention to the heat. They were excited to explore their surroundings with new friends. They packed water and peanut butter and grape jelly sandwiches in their backpacks and headed out to see all the sights.

The library, the school, the city park, and the courthouse were noted as they walked through town. Nothing seemed very exciting that morning.

"Isn't this the town where a UFO is supposed to have landed?" asked Gabriel. "I'd like to see that."

"Me, too," said Emma.

Kimi and Ben exchanged glances.

"We're not supposed to go there," said Kimi.

"That's right," said Ben. "It's off limits."

"You mean they have guards?" asked Gabriel.

"No," said Ben. "There are signs posted, and our parents tell us to keep out."

"Then let's go and look around," said Gabriel. "Who's going to know?"

"Please," said Emma.

Finally, Ben and Kimi sighed and gave in.

"It's out by the old, deserted mission," said Kimi. "about a twenty-minute walk."

"Then let's get started," said Emma.

The walk wasn't as easy as Gabriel and Emma thought it would be, but they never considered the walk back.

By the time the friends reached the old mission, they were hungry and thirsty. They sat in the shade of a crumbling wall and ate and drank. As they began to feel refreshed, they started to look around.

Most of the old church was gone now. Just two of the former walls were standing. Weeds had grown inside where the floor used to be.

"Did people stop coming to church here after the UFO landed?" asked Emma.

"No," said Ben, "it had been abandoned for some time before that. A new church in town drew all the members away from here. It was more convenient. My mom says that time and weather took its toll on this old mission."

"What about the UFO landing?" asked Gabriel. "When did it happen?"

"It was about ten years ago," Kimi answered. "At the time, we were too young to know what happened, of course. But we heard about it all the time when we were growing up.

"The story goes that one night, the sky lit up, just like a bright sunny day. It woke almost everybody up, and they ran out of their houses to see what was happening. All they could see was this UFO of some sort with a huge ray of light hovering over the old mission.

"A lot of people jumped in their cars and tried to go out there, only the cars wouldn't start. Not one of them could move until the UFO took off, straight up into the sky and out of sight.

"The cars started then, and almost everybody in town ended up out here. There was nothing much to see by the time they got here. The earth was disturbed in one place by the mission's foundation. It looked like something had been buried there. A few people wanted to investigate, but the others persuaded them to wait until morning so they could see better in daylight."

"What did they find the next morning?" asked Emma.

"That's another weird thing," said Ben. "They didn't find anything. The earth was back in place, just like it had been before."

"What do you think was buried? Did they come back and take it away?" asked Gabriel.

"I don't think so," said Kimi. "I think it is still here."

"Wow!" said Emma. "What do you think it is?"

"I don't know, but I've thought about it a lot," said Ben. "I think it might be some kind of time capsule. You know that people put time capsules in building foundations all the time so people can see what was important when they open them in the future."

"Maybe they are coming back someday, and this is some kind of device to test the atmosphere to see if they could survive or record changes in the environment," Gabriel suggested.

"That's possible," said Kimi.

"Let's look for it," said Emma, getting to her feet and looking at the foundation.

"People who have searched the area have had bad luck," warned Kimi. "One died, and another person went crazy. People say this place is cursed."

"Oh, people tell stories like that to keep kids like us away," said Gabriel. "There's nothing dangerous here in broad daylight! We might as well take a look around while we're here."

"Well, I suppose it wouldn't hurt," said Ben.

The four kids dropped their backpacks on the ground and began to examine the earth beside the foundation.

"Look at this," said Gabriel. "There is a sunken spot here in the back. Too bad we didn't bring a shovel to dig around."

"These sharp rocks will do," said Kimi, picking up two rocks that once were a part of the mission wall.

The friends took the rocks and started scraping away dirt from the sunken hole. Then it happened. Gabriel hit something that clanked like he had hit metal!

The kids dug harder and exposed a long cylindrical container made of some kind of hard surface that none of them recognized!

"Look!" said Emma. "It has some writing on it!"

The children knelt down closer.

"It is a time capsule," said Kimi. "You're right, Emma. There is writing!"

"And it's in English!" said Ben.

"This is too weird!" said Gabriel. "It has today's date on it. It's supposed to be opened today."

"Somebody must be playing a trick on us," said Emma.

"Nobody knew we were coming out here," said Ben. "How could anyone play a trick?"

"Our parents probably figured we would come," Emma said.

"I don't think it's a trick," said Gabriel. "Nobody has any kind of container like this. And it looks like it has been in the ground for a long time. I think we should go tell our parents."

"Yes," agreed Emma. "Our dad is a colonel. He'll know what to do."

They thought for a minute, nodded their heads in agreement, picked up their backpacks, and hurried back to town.

Far out in space, an alien leader activated a timing device inside the time capsule. Slowly, it opened and out flew thousands of tiny creatures seeing their new environment for the first time. They flew off in all directions to grow and multiply.

In countries all over the world, time capsules were opening, and creatures like these at the base were joining the others.

In town, Colonel Nicolas Workman listened and smiled as the children told their story.

"Somebody must have buried it there as a joke," he said. "We'll drive out later this afternoon and take a look."

He chuckled when the children left to explore the rest of the town. *Kids today have such imaginations,* he thought. *The unbelievable things they conjure up!*

Unfortunately, not even an experienced military man like Colonel Nicolas Workman would expect a world invasion on such a bright summer day.

Fireflies

It was a southern summer night, and the people up and down the quiet streets of Echo Creek were sitting on their front porches drinking lemonade and tea, making casual conversation, and watching fireflies. They had no idea that life was not nearly as safe as it seemed.

The fireflies looked like thousands of little light dots coming from the sky. They were flying low to the ground, which meant, according to local weather lore, that rain was coming soon.

Hannah Claiborne was spending the night with Lily Tanaka, and they had brought out glass fruit jars with holes punched in the lids so they could catch fireflies.

When the jars were full enough, the girls would walk down the street beyond the streetlights and let the fireflies light the jars like little lanterns to drive back the dark—if only for a very short time. After a little while, they would open the jars and let them go.

"Aren't the fireflies beautiful, Momma?" asked Lily.

"Oh, yes," Mrs. Tanaka replied. "We used to call them lightning bugs when I was a little girl. I think I like fireflies better."

"Be sure that the holes in the lid are big enough for air to get in," said Mr. Tanaka. "We wouldn't want the fireflies to die."

"We made the holes big enough, Mr. Tanaka," said Hannah. "My friend Theo says that fireflies are very important. We mustn't kill them. He says they light the way for little elves to find their way home in the darkness to the hollow trees where they live. And they light the way home for fairies who love to dance under toadstools."

"I'm sure that's true," smiled Mr. Tanaka.

"Wonder why they don't burn themselves when they light up?" asked Hannah.

"I think the light comes from some chemical combination that can produce light with almost no heat," said Mrs. Tanaka. "I don't think our scientists produce light that way."

"Come on, Hannah," said Lily. "Let's go see how many we can catch."

The girls ran about the yard catching fireflies and putting them in their jars. They had such fun that nobody thought about how the fireflies felt. Nobody ever wondered what those flashes of light, like little cameras, really meant. And on this southern summer night, the people of Echo Creek and the rest of the world took life for granted.

The two girls finished collecting fireflies and headed down to the darkness beyond the streetlights as they often did on summer nights.

The fireflies settled down in the jars to wait for their release. They were frightened at first when they were captured, but they had learned that after a few minutes, they were usually released. They rarely suffered a casualty now.

Hannah and Lily sat on the curb and held up their jars to watch them light up.

"You know, Hannah," said Lily, "sometimes, when I see the fireflies light up, I think I see stars way up in the sky flash back!"

"Maybe they do," said Hannah. "I sometimes wonder if fireflies come from another world."

Hannah and Lily would never know how close they were to the truth.

Inside the jars, the fireflies were getting restless. They had a lot of work to accomplish, and they needed to be free to do it. The girls noticed that they were more active than usual.

"They are flying against the glass," said Hannah. "They don't usually do that. Do you think they need to get out?"

"I don't know," said Lily. "They are acting funny."

"Maybe we should go ahead and let them go," suggested Hannah. "I've never seen them act so anxious."

"Yeah, I think we should release them," said Lily.

She opened up her jar and let them go. Hannah did the same.

"Did you ever notice that their flashes make some kind of pattern?" asked Lily. "Maybe they are sending messages?"

"Who would receive a message from a firefly?" laughed Hannah.

"I don't have an answer for that," laughed Lily. "Let's go back to the house. I have a new game I want to show you."

The girls walked from the darkness, under the street-lights, and back to the front porch of Lily's house.

"Dad, do you think fireflies send signals?" Lily asked.

"I think they send signals to find mates," he answered.

Lily didn't pursue the subject. She and Hannah went inside to play a new game.

Mr. and Mrs. Tanaka sat on their deck, sipped their sweet tea, and watched the stars twinkling far, far away.

"I know it sounds crazy," said Mrs. Tanaka, "but sometimes I think the stars look like they are blinking a message."

"I wouldn't go around saying that to anyone," laughed Mr. Tanaka. "People will think you're batty."

"I suppose so," she replied, "but I get the feeling that some catastrophe is coming that we ought to know about."

"Well, if it is," he said, "it is probably too late to do anything about it now. Let's forget about it and go to bed."

While people all over the world slept like those in Echo Creek, the fireflies frantically flashed their little cameras and transmitted pictures across the vast universe to their base planet. The pictures were received, analyzed, cataloged, and carefully stored.

"Hurry!" said the leader to the other fireflies. "We need to get as many pictures transmitted as we can before the rain comes in."

They hurried as directed.

"Do you think we can complete our mission in time?" asked a young firefly.

"I hope so," replied another. "We can only recreate what we photograph and send back to our base. And it's common knowledge that these earthlings will destroy their planet very soon."

The little fireflies fell silent, but their camera flashes filled the night, trying to complete their assignment before the hate, weapons of destruction, and all the violence erupted to end the world.

Swampers

Miss Mimi's was the most popular diner near Cold Water Swamp. It attracted all the locals, plus the tourists that passed by on their way to Cold Water Resort several miles down the road. They all came for Miss Mimi's specialty, which was the best fried frog legs in the south!

Miss Mimi depended on three swampers—Leah Fahrat, Clarence Williams, and Hudson Stevens—to keep her supplied with the best frog legs anywhere. They never let her down, because frog hunting was a joy to them, not a job.

It was getting dusky dark when the three swampers came into the diner and ordered a platter of frog legs and drinks to wash them down.

"I'm getting low on frog legs, froggers," Miss Mimi told them when she brought their order to the table. "Do you think you can bring me some tomorrow?"

"You've got it!" said Leah. "Tonight will be a good night for frog hunting."

"Fog is rolling in," Miss Mimi commented. "I wouldn't like to be out frogging tonight."

"That's because you are not a night creature," laughed Hudson. "We are like bats, vampires, and owls! We come out when the sun goes down! We are true swampers!"

Everybody laughed, and several customers copied the swampers' orders for frog legs and drinks. The diner was bright and cheery in contrast to the outside where complete darkness had now settled in. The swampers finished off the frog legs and told everybody they would see them the next day.

"Look out, frogs," warned Leah, laughing. "Here we come! We want your legs! We want your legs!"

They walked outside into a drastic change in surroundings. The fog wasn't as heavy as they had thought, but the air was damp and chilling. For one minute, Clarence just stood there, looking back at the brightly lit diner and feeling like he should go back inside and skip frog hunting tonight.

"What's the matter with you?" Hudson turned around and asked. "Are you coming or not?"

"I'm coming! I'm coming!" he told him.

"Well, hurry it up," said Hudson. "We don't have all night."

A chill shook him as he joined his two friends in Hudson's old truck. In a few minutes, they had left the truck by the dock where they kept their fourteen-foot, flat-bottomed motorboat. They climbed in and slid silently into the sinister waters of the swamp.

They navigated a series of canals that led to one of the most productive spots for frog catching. They used their headlamps to scan the banks for the huge bullfrogs that were generally there in abundance. The frogs did not get wind of their presence, so the swampers had thirty-eight keepers in under two hours.

"These will fry up tasty!" said Leah. "We might as well call it a night."

Clarence turned the boat toward home, but something caught his eye as the beam of light from the headlamps focused on the largest bullfrog he had ever seen.

"Would you look at that," he whispered to his two companions.

Leah and Hudson looked where he was pointing. They couldn't believe the size of the bullfrog they were seeing.

"How did we miss that one?" asked Leah.

It stared back at the swampers unafraid. Its eyes had a gleam they had never seen before.

"I don't think that one will ever be caught," said Clarence. "It looks like something that has lived here since time began."

It stared for a few seconds more before merging with the shadows along the bank. It made one sound, which was more like a growl than a croak.

The three swampers shivered and did not speak again until Clarence pulled up to the dock. They loaded the catch into the truck and drove to Leah's place. There they cut off the frogs' legs and threw the bodies into the woods for the raccoons to feast on.

All three felt some unseen presence staring at them from the swamp, and it made them nervous.

They took their delivery to Miss Mimi's diner but were not in their usual good spirits when she paid them for the frogs.

"Anything wrong, frog hunters?" she asked.

They assured her everything was fine, but they did not stick around to visit like they usually did. Something deep inside each swamper was warning them to go home as quickly as they could. Miss Mimi felt uneasy, too, and quickly put the frog legs away.

The inhabitants of Cold Water did not sleep well that night. The three swampers tossed and turned and couldn't get comfortable. Splashing sounds and distant croaks made them fearful in a way that they had never felt before.

Miss Mimi, who always liked to sleep with her window open to hear the night sounds, got up after a few minutes and closed and locked the window. For some reason, the sounds were menacing tonight, and she couldn't explain why. Twice she thought she heard something fling itself against her window in her second floor apartment over the diner.

When she finally fell asleep, she had a terrible nightmare. Bloody frog bodies squirmed their way into her kitchen. Frog legs sizzling in her frying pans jumped out and reattached themselves to their bodies. Miss Mimi woke from her dream, sweating and screaming.

She tried to put the dream out of her mind as she prepared the items for her daily menu. The fried frog legs were a big hit as usual. She texted the three swampers and asked them to supply her with more.

They reluctantly agreed and set out to fill Miss Mimi's order.

Something must have happened in the swamp last night, she thought. *My swampers are not acting like themselves.*

Hours passed, and Miss Mimi worried that something had happened to them. When they didn't make their delivery at the usual time, Miss Mimi went on to bed.

"They'll be here early in the morning," she assured herself.

That night, Miss Mimi dreamed that a huge bullfrog was sitting on her bed, staring at her face. Again, she awoke screaming, but her room was silent and empty. She hurried down to the kitchen but found it silent and empty, too. The swampers had not made the promised delivery. She didn't know what to think. They were her friends, and she suddenly feared for their safety.

Morning came slowly, as if it had news it did not want to deliver.

"What am I going to serve today?" Miss Mimi asked herself. "I have no frog legs! It's the first time I haven't had them on the menu."

When the clock hands turned to opening time, customers joined Miss Mimi in her concern for the swampers. They agreed that it was time to call the police.

The police chief and one of his sergeants arrived at the diner and tried to calm everybody down.

"They know that swamp like the back of their hands, so they're probably out there somewhere having fun. I can't imagine foul play or that they would get lost," he said. "My sergeant and I will go check it out and let you know."

The hours passed slowly. The sun was out, but the mood in the diner got darker and darker. Finally, a police car pulled into the diner parking lot. Everybody who had waited around rushed outside, too anxious to wait for the news.

The police chief's face had a tinge of green like he had been very sick to his stomach.

"I just sent my sergeant for the coroner," he said. "I think we should all go inside. Miss Mimi, I could use a cup of your strongest black coffee."

With the coffee cup in his hand, the police chief told what he and his sergeant had found in the swamp.

"We followed the channels they usually follow," he said, "and we came to the spot where they typically catch the most frogs. We looked around and didn't see them, but then we smelled something cooking. We spotted a small fire on the bank, so we went to investigate."

He stopped at that point, drank a swallow of coffee, and almost gagged.

After a moment he continued.

"We tied up our boat and climbed the bank," he told them, "Neither of us could believe what we saw in front of us. A little fire was burning, and around it were six roasted human legs. Even though the bodies were missing, there was no doubt whose legs they were. You just can't imagine the sight. Nothing like that ever made either of us as sick in our lives!"

"Oh, goodness," said Miss Mimi. "How could such a thing happen?"

"I can't believe it myself," said the police chief, "so I'll understand if you don't believe me. But we looked among the bushes along the banks, and there were rows of bullfrogs staring at us! In the front was the biggest bullfrog you could possibly imagine; he was the size of two or three men. We stared back for a few seconds and froze; we were just too horrified to move. Then that big frog croaked and flicked out its tongue. On it we saw a human hand!"

"What did you do?" one of the listeners yelled.

"We came to our senses and we ran!" said the police chief. "I can tell you that I am not going back in there again! Men and women braver than me are going to have to bring back what's left of those swampers. That was warning enough for me!"

Miss Mimi agreed. It was warning enough for her, too. Now tourists and locals see a sign on the diner that reads, "Miss Mimi's Famous Pancake House!" No frog legs or swampers were ever mentioned again!

Beyond the Legend

Madison Watson loved holidays. Her favorite gift last June for her birthday was a book, *Holiday Legends*. She had read it twice from cover to cover.

"I want to check these out," Madison told her parents. "I want to find out if the stories are really true."

"These are just stories," said her dad.

"And there are some things that are not for us to know," said her mom. "Sometimes, it's nice to have some unknown elements in our lives. Let life have some wonder in it."

"I like to figure out mysteries," said Madison.

"Well, I guess that's not a bad thing if that is really what you like to do," said her dad.

"I wonder about chime children, born on the stroke of midnight between Christmas Eve and Christmas," she said. "Do you think they can really see ghosts?"

"Maybe," said her dad, "but I don't know any chime children."

"What I really want to know is whether animals can talk at midnight on Christmas Eve and if the dead can rise from their graves on that night and walk without leaving tracks," said Madison.

"Some things are best left alone," said her mom. "I don't want you exploring Aunt Gwen's barn when we go to spend the holidays with her this year!"

"Oh, Mom!" protested Madison. "Why not? She keeps animals in her barn, and she lives near a graveyard!"

"I don't want you going to the graveyard, either," said her dad.

"But, Dad! Aunt Gwen's farm would be the perfect place to explore!" said Madison. "You could go with me."

"Not me," said her father, "I'm going to have a delicious meal, hang my stocking, and get a good night's rest."

"We could at least stay up and wait for Santa," said Madison.

"No," said her mom. "If he catches us, he might leave coal in our stockings!"

Madison was at the age when she was sorting through information about Santa, fairies, ghosts, and goblins.

Why can't people just tell the truth? she thought. *Why do stories have to conflict with each other? If I can't trust adults to tell me the truth, then I'll have to find the truth on my own. Aunt Gwen's is a good place to start. Dad and Mom don't need to know about the things I'm planning.*

Madison was excited when the day finally arrived for them to visit Aunt Gwen. The car was loaded down with board games and the things they would need during the trip. Madison packed her book, *Holiday Legends.*

The ride up to Aunt Gwen's farm was very pleasant. The snow had arrived during the night, and children were already out with their sleds. There were frozen ponds where children were already venturing out to skate. Madison enjoyed the winter scenes, but she was much happier when she saw the graveyard and Aunt Gwen's barn.

Aunt Gwen was delighted to see them. She had stayed on at the farm after Uncle Monroe had died last summer. She said he would want them to celebrate Christmas together as usual, so she had put up the decorations they had always used.

The four of them unloaded the car and unwrapped the food in the kitchen. Madison had a feeling that this Christmas would be like no Christmas she had ever celebrated before.

She joined her parents and aunt at a table filled with every holiday treat she could think of. After dinner, Aunt Gwen played the piano, and they all sang carols. Madison and her parents built a cozy fire in Aunt Gwen's fireplace. Then they all went to bed a little after eleven o'clock.

Madison struggled to stay awake so she could carry out her plan. When she saw the clock and realized it was eleven forty-five and only a few minutes before midnight, she quietly got out of bed. She put her pillows under her cover so it would look like she was in bed asleep. She took her watch and small flashlight so she could know when midnight came.

She had slept in her clothes, so now she only had to put on her boots, hat, coat, and gloves, and slip out her window.

The moonlight was bright, but she kept to the shadows as much as possible so she wouldn't be seen. She entered the barn and kept away from the animals' stalls so they wouldn't see her. She sat quietly and watched the minutes tick away.

Then the atmosphere changed. One star beamed much brighter than the rest, and the air was charged with energy!

And then the legend came to life. As Madison saw the hands on the clock reach twelve, a miracle happened. The animals started to speak!

"Moo-moon is bright," said the cow.

"Yes," agreed the others.

"Gather 'round," said one of the horses. "We need to discuss what's going to happen next year."

The animals did as the horse said, with the sheep following last.

"One death is coming soon," said the donkey.

This shocked Madison. She stepped from her hiding place.

"Who is going to die?" she asked the animals.

The animals were very disturbed by her presence. They all began to speak at the same time.

"No humans should ever hear us talk!"

"No!"

"Get out!

"No," she answered. "I want to know who is going to die!"

"It is the worst of luck to the one who hears us speak," said the horse. "We know things that humans are never meant to know in advance."

"Like what?" asked Madison.

"Once you hear us talk, you can never again talk to humans," said the donkey.

"You heard us, so now you have a problem!"

"What do you mean?" asked Madison, suddenly feeling scared. "What problem are you talking about?"

"You can never see your family again!" said the cow.

"Of course I will!" she shouted. "You can't keep me here! I'm going right now, and you can't stop me."

The animals bowed their heads as Madison ran out the door!

Outside, Madison ran toward the house. She didn't notice that a patch of ice was by the side of the barn. She slipped and fell, hitting her head hard on the ice. She blacked out for a minute, but when her head cleared, she saw a man coming down from the graveyard. She ran toward the man.

"Help me get home!" begged Madison. "The animals just told me that I can never see my family because I heard them talk. Is that right?"

"I am afraid it is," said the man. "You meddled with powers you did not understand."

"I just wanted to know if the animals could talk and if the dead could walk on Christmas Eve," said Madison. "I know about the animals now, but what about the walking dead? Can they walk on Christmas Eve?"

"Well, let me put it this way," said the man. "I am your Uncle Monroe! It's Christmas Eve, and we are both walking now."

It took a minute, but then the truth sunk in. Madison saw herself and the man floating just above the ground, leaving no tracks as they headed for the graveyard.

About the Author

Roberta Simpson Brown is known by her fellow writers as the "Queen of the Cold-Blooded Tales" for good reason. Her chilling ghost stories take place in familiar, contemporary settings: family rooms, farms, campgrounds—with an undercurrent of something very, very scary pulling the reader into the undertow of terror. She grew up on a farm near Russell Springs, Kentucky, at the edge of Appalachia. Stories she heard there as a child and at Berea College as a student made her realize the importance of preserving great stories and passing them along for future generations.

Roberta has appeared from coast to coast at parks, workshops, schools, libraries, institutions including the National Middle School Conference, and The Corn Island Storytelling Festival. She has written for *Louisville Magazine*, and has performed on radio and television (*National Public Radio* and *Voice of America*) and The Kentucky Center for the Arts. She was even featured telling her own stories on Lifetime Television's show, "Beyond Chance."

She has been a featured author at the Southern Festival of Books in Nashville, the National Storytelling Festival in Tennessee, the Kentucky Book Fair, and the Southern Festival of Books at Bowling Green, Kentucky. Roberta retired from teaching to devote full time to her writing and storytelling. She spends her free time reading, walking, watching videos of her favorite classic TV show "Emergency!" and working for animal rights. She lives in Louisville with her husband Lonnie, who is very supportive of her work and who "keeps the bad things away." Roberta and Lonnie do paranormal investigations with the Louisville Ghost Hunters and The American Ghost Society.